I0545256

A Quidell Brothers
ROMANCE

I'd been a mirror, I think, to protect myself. Maybe also to hide. But I can't now. Touching forces me out from behind my glass wall and I whisper his name. "Tom."

"Sammie." His hand curls into my hair and his stomach suddenly pulls away from me. A kiss takes my mouth, hot and intense. Once again, he pulls the poison from my body....

THOMAS'S MUSE

Quidell Brothers Book One

KRIS AUSTEN RADCLIFFE

Six Love Erotic Romance

THE WORLDS OF
KRIS AUSTEN RADCLIFFE

Northern Creatures Box Set One: Books 1-3
Northern Creatures Box Set Two: Books 4-6

THOMAS'S MUSE

A Quidell Brothers
ROMANCE

By
Kris Austen Radcliffe

Six Love Erotic Romance
Minneapolis

www.krisaustenradcliffe.com

Copyright 2018 Kris Austen Radcliffe
All rights reserved.

Published by
Six Love Erotic Romance

Edited by Annetta Ribken
Copyedited by Juli Lilly
Cover to be designed by Kris Austen Radcliffe
Plus a special thanks to my Proofing Crew.

Copyright notice: All rights reserved under the International and Pan-American Copyright Conventions. No part of this book may be reproduced or transmitted in any form or by any means, electronic or mechanical, including photocopying, recording, or by any information storage and retrieval system, without permission in writing from the publisher.

This is a work of fiction. Names, places, characters and incidents are either the product of the author's imagination or are used fictitiously, and any resemblance to any actual persons, living or dead, organizations, events, programs, services, or locales is entirely coincidental.

Warning: the unauthorized reproduction or distribution of this copyrighted work is illegal. Criminal copyright infringement, including infringement without monetary gain, is investigated by the FBI and is punishable by up to 5 years in prison and a fine of $250,000.

For requests, please e-mail: publisher@sixtalonsign.com.

Second print edition, June 2018
Version: 11.3.2022

ISBN: 978-1-939730-58-9

THOMAS'S MUSE

A Quidell Brothers
ROMANCE

Special thanks to my dear husband Peter for being the inspiration for all the good men.
Also a special thanks to Katie for helping with so many things, the least of which being titles and names.
And finally, an added thanks to Netta and Terry, who polish what I dig out of my psyche. I also want to also thank Kami, Jonel, Kristine, and everyone else who, from the beginning, believed in my stories.
Thank you!

CHAPTER 1

Samantha

The first moment I thought *Maybe I need to get my own place* wasn't when I tripped over Rick's bike for the thousandth time. Or when the ripe smell of workout clothes and dirty dishes hit my nose as I opened the apartment door, either. Or when I sneezed. No, none of that.

Rick's an athlete—triathlons, races, modeling to make ends meet because the sponsorship deals haven't quite come through—and he treats it like a career. An investment banker-like, cutthroat, "I work hard so give me my damned Mercedes" career.

The rest of his life sits unwashed and collecting dust.

Making me sneeze.

I knew what I was in for eight months ago when I moved into the spacious wonder of Rick's touched-by-an-architect loft. Into his world of boom and bust. It's exhilarating—I won't lie. When he's up, he's *up*. And he's good at celebrating.

At the time, I thought it a worthwhile trade-off. I received every inch of Rick's scrumptious hardness, a downtown life, and escape from the tired suburban trajectory I'd been born into. But now his bike rattles when I knock it with the door, the place smells like bachelor, and he even closed the curtains before he left.

Shadows force the sunlight onto the rough brick of the loft's walls, making it look like old skin. This place is solid, much like Rick. Sinewy and hard and cut along perfect lines. It's an old refurbished warehouse and it has character.

But it doesn't have soul. And I finally figured out why.

We have no art. Or, more precisely, *he* has no art. No cheap single-man prints. No family snapshots in nice frames. Not one giant narcissistic photo from a modeling gig. The apartment has nothing but a cat who is as bland as the walls.

And deep inside, I wonder what that really means.

Thomas

IT'S TIME FOR ME TO MOVE OUT OF MY BROTHER'S BASEMENT.

My stomach tightens, thinking about it. He did a good job renovating before his ex did her crazy bitch dance and ran off. It's open and sunny, for a lower level. Good light streams in from the big rear windows. I'll miss painting in the warm afternoon glow reflecting off his golden patio out back.

I never wanted to live in his basement, but he needed help with his kid. I needed a place to crash while I finished school. So I cooked mac and cheese for my nephew on the nights Daddy got called into work.

It's the least I could do.

And the kid loves posing. I've covered more canvases than I can count with sweet cherubs and little superheroes.

Right now, a long line of action figures, stuffed toys, books, and video game boxes snakes across the floor of my "studio," running from the steps to the living room upstairs into the box my nephew packs my paints. Bart is quite reverent of my supplies, for a four-year-old.

He holds up a tube of vermillion, his shoulders square, and speaks to his army. "Apples," he says, and nods once before placing it in the box.

I watch, wondering. He asked wide-eyed if he could pack my paints, like it was the most important thing in the world. No way could I say no.

He picks up a tube of indigo, stares at it for a moment, and mouths the label, sounding out the word. "Almost night!" He looks proud.

I squat next to him and squeeze his shoulder. His ever-present superhero costume crinkles under my fingers and he looks up at me, a bit glassy-eyed.

"What are you doing, little man?" He makes rivers of toys all the time, so that's not new, but color naming is.

"I remember the colors, Uncle Tommy. When you used them." He holds up a tube of yellow and points to a summer portrait I painted of him a couple of weeks ago. It hangs on the wall, next to the stairs, in a spot bright in the morning sun.

I don't know what to say, though I remember doing the same thing when I was his age. Lining up my toys. Making patterns on the floor. I drew and drew and taped my stuff to the walls so I could watch the light play over my crayon colors.

I'd seen Bart stare at his markers, his nose crinkled like they weren't *right*. As if they didn't have the scent he expected a color to have.

I give him a hug. "I'm going to miss you." I'll miss my brother too, but I need room. Dating is impossible when you live in your brother's basement. Sex while my nephew lives upstairs seems wrong on so many levels that the elevator between each floor of wrongness is itself wrong.

So I've been unofficially celibate for my last two years of undergraduate studies. It's been... tough.

Bart's eyes widen again. "When will you be home?"

He's got a special scent, one I can only assume is what little boys smell like. He's the only one I know, so I can't say for sure. But he sort of smells like my brothers. And me, I suppose. It's not attractive, just family. "I'll come visit, okay?"

My new place is closer to downtown, not far from my new job. I'm just thankful to have work. I know a lot of people my age who moved home after graduation.

"Uncle Robby says you're selling monster food." Bart blinks, his eyes wide again. It's amazing what kids hear, when adults speak.

My younger brother, Rob, scoffed when I told him about the job in the art department of one of the big multi-national food corporations. Called me a sell-out.

The beers flowed that afternoon on the deck, now that Rob is legal. He chewed his burger and said the last thing he expected was for me to be drawing happy pictures of frankenfood and GMO yogurt. Bart must have heard him.

But it's a job and jobs paid the rent.

"Tell you what," I say. "I'll draw you some 'monster food.'" I curl my fingers and growl, tickling his belly.

Bart screeches, his plastic costume wrinkling. "Uncle Tommy!" He lets loose a little four-year-old-boy fart and screeches some more.

I roll around on the floor with him, laughing. He'll be okay. Little Bart, he's just like my brother, except for the farting. Dan's the biggest and the best of the three of us.

And like my brother, I hope to do the best I can, with what I've got.

CHAPTER 2

Samantha

Andy leans against my cubicle's overhead bin and looks down at me with his baby blues. The metal groans when he crosses his arms. His well-sculpted biceps strain his perfectly-pressed button-down and I swear the fabric groans too. I tell him to call Rick's agent but he just smirks and says he likes his job here in our wide-open land of cubicles, usually with a flourish and a wink.

Andy, my usual lunch mate and the best work-husband a girl could want.

"Let's see them." He wiggles his fingers in front of my face.

Andy's had a crush on Rick since we started dating. Not a *real* crush—more like a supportive best friend showing approval—but he does enjoy the photographic evidence that I am, in fact, living with a hot hunk of man model.

Who took a cab to the airport this morning for another photo shoot, after I left for work. He hadn't really talked to me, not even to ask me to take care of the cat.

"I didn't bring any," I say to Andy. Rick didn't *share* share—he sent me a link with the equivalent of *lucky you* in the subject line. I didn't print them, either. This time, I didn't even load the shots onto my phone. I know he was being snarky, but *lucky me*, indeed.

Shaking my head, I point at my monitor. "Work. Deadline." Honestly, I don't want to think about Rick right now.

Andy rolls his eyes and the walls of my cubie groan again when he stands up straight. Sometimes I forget how tall he is. "You write press releases in your sleep."

"It's not a press release. Product testing." Every year, our company prototypes new cereals, yogurts—anything in garish packaging they can slap with a "good for you" logo and call "healthy." It's a complicated process involving several departments, including ours.

"Ah." Andy's nose wrinkles when he nods at my monitor. There are aspects of our work he likes, and aspects he doesn't. Just like me. That's why he's a wonderful work-husband.

He keeps his arms crossed as he turns to go. "Oh!" He lifts his hand off his elbow and twirls his finger in the air like a magician. "I have noon meetings all week so you'll need to find some other sucker to lunch with you." He winks.

Guess I'll eat my frozen boxes of well-tested midday meal product alone this week. I nod toward my computer. "Probably be at my desk, anyway."

My entire cubie rattles when he wraps his fingers around the top edge of the wall. "Don't do that. It's supposed to be nice. At least take your tablet and go outside." He frowns like a big brother, or an uncle, or a father.

"Yes, Dad." I frown back.

Andy laughs and shakes his head full of perfectly cut, chocolate brown hair. He really should call Rick's agent.

"Back to work, you slacker." He walks off, toward his own cubie. "Next time, pictures!" he calls over his shoulder.

My chair squeaks when I lean back, thinking about pictures, and I realize my cubicle is as ugly as Rick's loft. The gray-blue nylon fabric walls feel like they were textured to mimic office furniture, or burlap, or maybe someone's unfortunate Christmas sweater. They do their job —cutting neighbor noise and fading into the background while I work —but they're flat. And completely lack personality.

I've pinned up a few items: Pictures from a Museum of Modern Art calendar I bought a few years ago. A couple photos of Mr. Pickles —Mickles, I call him—Rick's sweet cat. A page or two out of one of the clothing catalogs featuring Rick and his picture-perfect ah-shucks smile. That's it. Nothing special. Nothing unexpected. Not even a plant.

My cubicle's door opens toward the windows, so at least I see daylight. The tint on the glass turns the morning a weird green, but it's natural light. I can tell when it's time to eat and when it's time to leave, all by the pitch of the sun.

Maybe I should get a plant. Something living.

A message pops up on my screen: The boss wants me to go downstairs and pick up mock-ups from the Art Department. I stretch, leaning back to see past my cubicle door to the wall of industrial windows not far away.

It looks like a nice day. Bright, and not cave-like. Maybe I should go outside. But first, I need to pick up fresh new designs for America's freshest and newest breakfast foods.

The stairwell door hisses shut behind me as its hydraulic closer keeps it from slamming. The company recently painted the stairwell and my floor's door is purpleberry purple, a cereal box color so vividly bright it looks like a monitor screen and not paint. The tangy, chemical stink of "low odor" paint also lingers. I rush down, trying not to breathe too deeply.

The standard big building metal and concrete stairs clunk as I jog, and my skirt rubs against my legs. Tight black pencil skirts and heels don't make the best running gear, but I try to take the "dress for success" bullshit to heart. The shoes, though, stay in my desk drawer when I leave for home each evening. Bus rides call for sneakers.

The door to the Art Department has a graffiti look, as if someone spray painted versions of all the company's product logos onto it. It's graphic design all the way, with very little "art." But it gets the point across. I pull open the door.

The windows are different down here. The day doesn't shine through weirdly green, like upstairs. It bursts into the wide open space, white and clear and warm. The entire floor is flooded with natural light

—and no cubicle farm messes it up, though cubies do line the inner wall next to me, on either side of the door. The Art Department prefers big tables and open spaces.

I walk in, breathing in deeply, and memories of my undergraduate days flood back. I took a lot of art courses, Art History mostly, and I spent my time in studios. They have a particular smell to them, an art-in-progress scent of dyes and metal and clay. Real tools, real media, and the hands of real people.

I loved it. I might marvel at what the Art Department here whips up with software, but nothing beats the sound of brushes on a canvas and the smell of paints.

There'd been this guy, too, my senior year. A tall, skinny kid with sandy brown hair and bright, pale eyes. I saw him once or twice, walking near the art building, a pad under his arm and a pack on his back. He moved around in a sort of awe, like a lot of freshmen, so I stayed away. At the time, I had a month before graduation and an eigh-teen-year-old boyfriend didn't seem like a good idea.

Sometimes I don't remember his face well, but I remember the look of his hands. And I imagine how they would have felt. How he would have smelled masculine but naïve, with a hint of charcoal from his work, if I had been smart enough to throw my reservations to the wind and come close. How he would have watched me in the morning light with his artist's eye, planning the next expression of his art.

I brush my fingers over the gray-blue nylon of the cubicle wall next to me. Time to retrieve mock-ups, not to pull up old fantasies, no matter how richly wonderful they are.

A body swings out of the cubicle—a big body with a wide chest and broad shoulders—and pulls up short, right in front of me.

"Oh!" pops from my mouth and I look up at the most wonderful blue-green eyes I have ever seen. Eyes more moving than Rick's. Beau-tiful eyes framed by thick, masculine lashes—not too long, but perfect for the shape of his face.

The man in front of me stands at least six inches taller, even with my heels. I get a good look at his strong jaw and expressive lips. Stubble covers his chin and I doubt he shaved this morning. His hair's messy too, as if he also forgot his comb. But his clothes are neat and clean, and he smells nice.

Quite nice, like real art, not the moused-over kind. Like texture and color and enough care to do it right. My forehead wrinkles. "Caring" didn't have a smell, but with this guy, it did. And it smelled brilliant, as if his potential reflected off his skin with the warm sunlight pouring through the window.

"Sorry," he says, grinning. One of his big hands grips the wall of his cubicle and it grumbles, much like mine does. His other reaches out to steady me, a reflex, I'm sure.

His hand cups my elbow. Strong, warm fingers grasp my flesh, not hard but with just enough pressure to steady me as I stagger back on my three inch heels.

"You okay? I didn't knock you, did I?" He watches me carefully, his gaze first searching my face before it drops for a quick glance at my chest. A tiny arch of approval moves from one eyebrow to the other before his eyes return to where they are supposed to look.

"No, no," I stammer. God, he's built like a man. Not Rick's obvious inverted triangle and twenty-six inch waist. No, this guy looks like he could pick me up and carry me out of a burning building while wearing full firefighter gear. He works, not trains.

His fingers release my elbow. "I didn't mean to startle you."

God, he has wonderful hands. Hands like the ones my remembered freshman would have now, four years out from my graduation. I look down at my arm, feeling, suddenly, as if I'd just been offered the best touch in the world and now he takes it away because he never should have offered it in the first place.

Then I remember the reason: Rick. I stand up straight, determined to regain my composure. I'm in a relationship and I need to act like it.

The new guy—because I'm damned sure I would remember him if I'd seen him before—smirks and looks away. As he shifts his weight, his hips move side to side in the centered way only men with strong abs and assured personalities move.

In this moment, as I stand no more than two feet from him, I know I'm blushing. I feel the heat move down my neck to my breasts and my nipples are so damned hard I'm *sure* they're showing though my bra. I'm starting to feel slick and I want to press my thighs together, but I don't. Because the blush is embarrassing enough.

He blinks a few times and I wonder if he can smell how much I want him, even though—God knows—I shouldn't. I wonder if he's going to turn me around right here and now, throw open the stairwell door, and back me against the ugly graphics on the door just so his fingers can find out for themselves in relative privacy what his sense of smell already knows.

Sometimes being horny all the time has its drawbacks. It's a plus, with Rick. When he's in town. And not too tired from training. Or too busy making sure his tan is just right or his chest is smoothly shaved. I stifle a frown, hoping the new guy won't think I'm frowning at him.

He's a gentleman. One obviously raised well, because he's fighting to keep his eyes on my face. I imagine he's holding in a growl, too. A deep baritone growl, one full of resonance from his huge chest.

He sticks out his hand. "My name's Thomas. Tom Quidell."

I wrap my palm around his, doing my best to be a gentlewoman. "Samantha Singleton. Sammie for short."

He winks and nods toward the door. "Do say, m'lady, from whence level of our dungeon of foodstuffs and factory numbers did you escape?"

I chuckle, smiling, thankful he's found a way to break the awkwardness, but his charm just makes me want him more. Which I *shouldn't*. The broken spell lets in a sudden and unwanted burst of guilt. I look away.

"Campaign Relations. I came down for—"

"Oh!" He snaps his fingers and backs into his cubie. "The mock-ups."

My body doesn't like that he's moved away. I feel a pull, as if I'm supposed to walk forward into the gap between his cubicle walls, so when he turns around again I'm right there, waiting for him to run into me, in full body contact.

A cardboard tube pokes out of the cubie, held in the air by his luscious hand. "My first." He winks again, his chest out, but he shoves his fingers into his pockets when I take the tube.

"When did you start?" I roll the tube between my hands, flipping it around like a wand. Why do *his* hands seem so familiar? Maybe it's because they're so masculine. And wonderful.

"Last week." He watches me, captivated. "I graduated Spring semester."

How could this huge, gorgeous man be a baby? Except he graduated, and was most certainly legal to drink. And no more than five years younger than me.

He turns back to his desk to grab something and I take in the square perfection of his backside. The man in front of me was definitely not a baby.

He holds out a card, a big smile lighting up his handsome face. "Just delivered this morning. You're the first."

I take the card, glancing at his name, title, office phone, and e-mail, knowing full well I will have it all memorized before I return to my floor. "A business card virgin, huh?" I tuck it into my pencil skirt's one pocket.

His face takes on a raw edge as he watches my hand smooth across my hip. I don't know if it's because I said "virgin" or because he likes what he sees. Or a combination of the two. But he catches his look quickly, like a true gentleman, and offers his hand once more. "Nice to meet you, Samantha Singleton, Sammie for short."

We shake again. I back toward the stairway door, watching him and not where I'm walking. A chuckle rolls from his cubie, but his phone rings, and he turns away.

So much for him following me into the stairway.

As I open the door I frown at myself, as indignant as I am embarrassed. I just met a good guy, a smart, sexy guy, and a gentleman. I live with someone. I sleep in the same bed with another man. And I'm flirting like some horny high schooler?

It's not the first time my libido has gotten me in trouble.

But part of me screams I need to pay attention. Would this temptation have occurred if the best part of my home life wasn't Mickles rubbing my ankles and demanding a good petting?

I stand in the stairwell for a long moment, wondering what to do.

Thomas

I JUST HANDED MY FIRST BUSINESS CARD TO THE HOTTEST WOMAN I have ever met in my entire life. Auburn hair so shiny it gleams. Hazel-green eyes sparkling with life. Full, round lips and the most beautiful smile I have ever seen.

Holy shit, I think, barely keeping my mind on the chatter coming at me over the phone. I write down a few things, say a few *ah-hahs* and ask for an e-mail confirming the conversation before I hang up. My brother Dan told me before I started to "always get an e-mail. Believe me, you *always* want an e-mail." Times like this, when all I can think about is getting into that tight little skirt to find what other tight little treats await me, I know my brother is a genius.

Sammie Singleton. I do a quick search in the company directory. An assistant to an assistant. Been with the company four years. Started here my sophomore year at the University.

So she's a little older than me. And has the lushest *real* breasts I ever wanted to rub my face between. Big, little, I don't care, but I like real. Fake looks fake. Fake feels fake. Some men don't care but I swear I can taste the silicone.

And her hips screamed *fuck me*. Pull up my black skirt and fuck me long and hard.

I close my eyes and force myself to count as I inhale. I can't get this worked up over a woman, especially one I just met. She could be married, for all I know. Or living with someone. If there's one thing I learned from Dan's divorce, it's to make sure you know who you are sleeping with.

CHAPTER 3

Samantha

I spend the rest of my day refusing to think about one Mr. Thomas, Tom Quidell. About his white shirt or the leather cord tied discretely around his neck. Or how soft his hair would feel between my fingers. Because every time I do, I see Rick standing in front of our bathroom mirror, a towel around his waist, as he checks out his chest stubble.

Watching Rick used to be the sexiest thing I could imagine. He'd come out of the shower and stare at me until I couldn't take it anymore and went down on him. I'd suck him off and he'd throw me onto the bed and fuck me missionary style.

At the time, it seemed so exotic. But now I wonder if it was just erotic.

And maybe not all that erotic, either. Maybe simply expected.

The bus bumps along the city streets and I look around at my fellow passengers. I've been riding this line, at this time, every day for eight months. In summer, it's bright outside and the morning dew covers the sidewalk. I wait at the stop, my bag in my hand and my sneakers on my feet, with the same three people. In the evenings, I ride home with a different set, a guy and two older women with their bags and their sneakers.

We take up our places but we don't talk to each other. Sort of like how I take up my place on my knees in front of Rick and don't know what it means to him.

Or what it means to me.

Inside, I wonder if there's any beauty to the movements of my life.

As I walk up the stairs to the loft, I remember, once again, Rick is gone on a shoot. This time, he's in L.A. He won't be back for four days.

I stop outside the door, my key in hand, and stare at the heavy wood slab. It's hung on massive iron hinges setting off its rough, original look. I think it must have been part of a worktable at some point, or maybe a floor. This door, it has history. And now it's trying something new.

I drop my bag on the floor and hit the light switch, even though there's enough evening light I should be able to see. But the curtains are closed. Rick must have shut them before he left this afternoon.

Flinging them open, I flood the loft with low sunlight. The main window faces west, and we're high enough in the building we see the sunset. Tonight, the sky spreads out red and gold, and lights up the world.

There's a piece of paper on the table, but I know what it says. Itinerary notes, flight numbers, and the unspoken reminder to feed Mickles. It's the same every time.

The cat prances around my legs, starved more for affection than for food. I pick him up and he rubs his soft fur against my cheek, purring and licking and meowing.

He might be a boring kitty, but he's a good boy. And he prefers the curtains open, just like me.

I set out his food and drop onto the couch. It crinkles as I lean back, its not-so-buttery leather muttering about my invasion of its domain. I pull a pillow under my head and look up at the solid beams crossing the ceiling. In the evening light, I see a few cobwebs, and wonder how to get the vacuum up there. Then I wonder if it's worthwhile.

My hand wanders to my thighs, as my mind wonders about other unknowns. I have a steady life with Rick, a good-ish life, but my brain's screaming *excitement! Possibilities! New new new!*

The handsome and huge Mr. Quidell.

I can't think about him anymore. I can't think about either man. So I dip back into my old fantasy, the one of the art student with his huge pad of paper under his arm.

He sits on the mound of lawn in front of the library, his pad propped against his pack. He's a puppy, tall and not quite filled out yet, with big hands and big feet. Bright, pale eyes watch me as I walk along between the buildings and the bike path. His gaze is intense, piercing, as if he likes what he sees. Wants what he sees.

On the couch, my hand pulls up my skirt and my thighs part. I end up here more often than I want to admit. Training makes Rick tired. Perfection comes at a cost, and usually it's our sex life.

I've gotten quite good at dealing with it on my own.

In the fantasy, I bite my lip, watching the gorgeous art student watch me. When I duck through the sliding doors into the library, his eyes narrow, and he's up off the grass, pad in one hand and pack in the other.

I duck through the second set of doors, into the library's cavernous lobby, glancing first to the left, then to the right. I need someplace private—a quiet corner to study. But I know he's right behind me, his tall stride long and purposeful. He'll follow. But how deep into the stacks will he go?

On the couch, my fingers find their private place, their quiet corner. I rub my clit lightly at first, feeling my fantasy self stride between shelf after shelf of books. In the fantasy, I want to rub myself, but I roll my hips instead, pushing my thighs together.

I know he's there. I know he's watching.

This part of the library has wide, tall windows, but it's a corner rarely visited. I stroke the spine of an old book, one untouched for ages, and I know I don't want to end up like it. Not in my fantasy, and not on my couch, where I wiggle.

He's there, at the other end of the long row of books, standing square to me, his pale eyes intense. The pack hangs from one of his hands, the pad from the other. His grip is strong, firm, and I wonder how those fingers will feel on my skin.

I back against an old metal desk, one that's been pushed into the forbidden corner of this forbidden section of the library. Sun streams in from the lone window behind it, but scattered by a rolling shelf full of books. I lean back into the dappled light, knowing my legs are parting and my nipples are pressing through my thin t-shirt.

On the couch, by myself, I sigh.

In the fantasy, he's right there in front of me, looking down at my face, his head slightly tilted. He drops the pack onto the desk on one side of me, but holds the pad.

He wants me to see.

The pages flip and then there's me. And me again. Walking. Smiling. My hand on my pack's straps. Another of me watching as the world passes by.

He's been drawing me for days. Weeks, maybe.

The pages turn again. Me, now in places I've never been. In a studio. On a bed I don't know. They are his fantasies. His desires.

Me, naked, reaching out to him.

His eyes intense, he closes the pad and drops it on the other side of me, trapping me between his possessions. The pad crinkles and a rustling breaks the silence.

He wants me. This beautiful boy wants me and he's been shy—too shy to say hello, but not shy enough to keep from drawing me on my back, nipples erect, his hope that I want him as much as he wants me blistering from the page.

In the fantasy I rub my hand over the bulge in his jeans. A groan rolls from his throat and he looks up at the ceiling. I see his smile.

Leaning forward, he reaches around my side to smooth the paper, his gaze locked to mine. I'm breathing hard, this close to him. He's gorgeous up close—thick sandy brown hair and beautiful blue-green eyes. I trace the leather cord tied around his neck.

When he leans toward me his shoulder brushes my breast and I gasp. He doesn't pull away, just stares at my chest, a hungry look making his young features seem older than he is.

"My muse," he says, his voice low and resonant. He may not have filled out yet, but his voice has. "You are *perfect*."

His mouth descends onto mine, searching and a little naïve. But he's strong and his stomach feels wonderful and rock hard under his shirt. I yank on the fabric, pulling it up to get a look at what my fingers feel.

"Take off the shirt." I say, rubbing my hands all over his skin.

He glances back into the library, but does as I say. His shoulders and arms do not disappoint. I rub cheeks and lips against his chest.

I'm so hot that when he tongues my mouth again, stealing my breath, I almost come. He chuckles, his hand moving under my skirt to my itty bitty panties, and a finger finds its way underneath.

"I want to see," he growls. "Let me see." His other hand yanks on my shirt as he backs away enough to see both my breasts and my pussy. He doesn't let go. I'd scream if he let go.

My fantasy man watches his finger dip in and out like he's never seen a woman's parts before. His other hand is working hard on my nipples, yanking and twisting, and I'm dying, it feels so good. He moves two fingers inside me and I'm bucking now, moaning, and his face is pure carnal joy. He likes how I react to him, and it just makes me want to fuck him more.

Just how he's looking at me makes me so horny I want to scream. The bulge in his jeans is too much and I unbuckle his belt, balancing carefully on the edge of the desk. He's cupping my pussy now, rubbing against my clit with the palm of his hand, and also keeping me from falling. His arms take all the work of holding me still, one hand working my fantasy clit the way my real finger works my real clit, the fingers of the other curled into the front of my bra. His biceps may be developing, but they are beautiful. A groan rolls from his throat, a deep groan, one urging me on. I work at it, but it takes effort to release his glorious cock from his boxer briefs. He's big—long and thick—and I can't believe my luck. Those hips are going to pound me hard and I'm going to come again and again.

I stroke him with a firm grip. He's hard—unbelievably hard—but his cock feels velvety and smooth. Wonderful. I roll my thumb over the tip, spreading his pre-cum, before licking the pad of my thumb.

God, my fantasy man tastes as good as he looks. Clean and wonderful and like a man who knows how to work.

His eyes narrow, his lids dropping, as he watches me suck at the pre-cum on the tip of my thumb. "Suck me," he demands, holding me where I am.

Oh, I think about it—how the crown of his cock will feel against my tongue. How taut his muscles will be as he tries to thrust into my mouth. How my throat will take all of him.

But this is my fantasy, not his. "You first." I widen my legs, leaning back. I want him to lick me. To taste and want to fuck me so bad he's gripping my hips enough it hurts.

His hand pulls off my pussy and cold air washes in behind it. Both hands pinch my nipples. Both flicking and squeezing and I let out a whimper. My pussy convulses, a pre-orgasm rippling up my belly. When he gets his tongue on me I'm going to come all over his face.

"Oh, God," I moan.

In my fantasy, his cock pushes into me. Hard.

On the couch, where I lay in the real world with my pencil skirt hitched up, I moan. Shudders flood from my contracting pussy all the way to my toes and my fluttering eyelids. I drop down, my fingers still rubbing. I'd forgotten the brilliance of this fantasy.

How much better it is than Rick's hard abs and his demanding stare.

I open my eyes. Mickles sits on the back of the couch, licking his paw like he doesn't care one bit what the human is doing.

I sit up even though all I want to do is take a nap, and think back to that last semester on campus. I spent a lot of time in and near the arts buildings as I finished off my last few classes and I remember my fantasy hottie and his pack and his artist's pad. Lots of students set up to draw passersby. He was one of many.

It dawns on me that the details of my fantasy could just be my new crush entering my desires. Maybe I added them this time. But no. Those details have always been there: pale eyes—blue-green in the bright sun—broad shoulders, even if they hadn't yet completely filled out, and the leather cord around his neck.

And the luscious hands.

I grab a pillow, suddenly so embarrassed I don't want anyone to see my face, not even Mickles.

And I realize why Tom seemed familiar.

All these years I've been using a memory to get myself off that, more often than not, worked better than thoughts of Rick. A memory of a hot guy I didn't know.

Until today.

CHAPTER 4

Thomas

I bounce my pen on my desktop—*snap, snap, snap*. My foot is going at the same rate—*tap, tap, tap*. And I've been semi-hard for three days, thinking about Ms. Sammie Singleton.

We crossed paths twice since she appeared on my cubicle threshold all sweet smelling and lickable. Both times she smiled and looked away and I wished I was better at reading people. Coy or embarrassed, I couldn't tell.

I think she's avoiding me, so the second time I stood my ground. "Do you want to have lunch today? It's nice out." I waved my hand at the weirdly green windows of her floor. They hazed Campaign Relations and everything within reach. Except her. They did nothing to cut her beauty.

She just blinked at me, not answering.

"Did I do something?" I didn't know what else to ask but I can't stand her not talking to me. It's driving me nuts.

She nodded and stood up straight, as if she'd decided to not be embarrassed anymore. Or coy. "No, no, of course not."

"Did *you* do something?" I grinned the most disarming grin I could, attempting to charm her out of whatever issue she's got going on.

For a long moment, she watched me with her hazel eyes, but she didn't answer my question. "Twelve fifteen? I'll meet you at the stairs by your cubicle?"

I got through. We made a lunch date.

That was at ten. The last two hours have been excruciating.

She's not wearing a ring, wedding or otherwise, so there's hope. And she's wearing another tight skirt today, a bright indigo number that screams *look at my hips*. And *look at my ass*. And her legs. And her waist.

Lunch better go well or I'll be punching holes in men's room walls.

I close down my illustrating program and push back my chair. The wheels do their squeaky pinging and it flows into my backside. Not a pleasant sensation against my balls.

Part of me wants to find a fuck buddy and work out all my pent-up issues over a few hours of itch scratching. Hook-ups serve a purpose, even if I've never liked the practice. There's something about not waking up with the person you went to bed with. I want to see a woman in the morning light, even if she doesn't always want to be seen.

Maybe I'm old fashioned.

It's twelve thirteen. I'll wait for her in the stairwell. Nothing beats watching a beautiful woman descend a staircase.

I push open the ugly door, absently wondering why someone thought the "graffiti" was a good idea. No sense of form, no flow, it looks like six or seven of the company's mascots threw up. I step into the landing, looking more at the lack of design in front of me than where I'm going.

"Tom!"

I look up. Sammie stands two steps up, her hand gripping the railing tight. Her gorgeous breasts are right there. Right at my eye level. So close all I need to do is walk one pace forward and bury my face in her chest.

She doesn't say anything. I blink, a sudden fear that I've been staring at her chest for minutes—*hours*—and next thing she's going to do is take a good strong swing and punch me right in the mouth.

But she doesn't. And when I look up at her face, she's wearing an expression I don't understand. Is she angry? Embarrassed? Disappointed?

Oh, shit, I think. How can I be this clueless with women?

"Ready for lunch?" She's tilted her head a little and looks away again. I wish I had better light than the buzzing fluorescent donut hanging in the center of the stairwell shaft.

I may paint this anyway. Sammie, the one bright spot of beauty against an ugly concrete backdrop.

She steps down to the landing. "When I was in school, the artists I hung around with all made that face." Her delicate finger swirls in front of my nose. "I called it the 'composition snarl.'"

I laugh, happy she's not going to smack me upside the head, like I deserve. Happy, too, she seems to like artists. "What did you major in?" We turn to walk down the remaining stairs to the first floor and the cafeteria, and I touch her back without realizing what I'm doing.

A tingle runs up my arm as I feel her muscles sway under my fingers. Shit, I could hold onto those hips all night, with her riding me.

I pull my hand back before she can get mad.

"Communications." She glances at my hand as I move next to her on the stairs.

I shove it into my pocket.

"Minored in Art History."

I smile. She becomes more and more perfect with each passing moment. We chat as we walk into the main lobby. I keep my hands in my pockets, trying to be a gentleman. It's difficult. All I want is more touches. More fingers along her back. To feel her skin. To see more smiles.

Her heels click on the granite floor and draw my eyes to her calves. Smooth, rounded, her legs look strong, like she works out.

In the cafeteria line she gets chicken salad and an orange, plus tea. Me, I get the same, but bigger, with a breadstick and two oranges.

At our table she snickers and wags her finger between the two pieces of fruit, an eyebrow up, another blush rising up her neck. "What's with the matching orange globes?"

I'm barely able to draw my gaze from the warm glow of her face. God damn I want to kiss her. Right now, right here in the company cafeteria in front of the entire staff. I feel myself harden and I glance away, down at my tray, trying to think about something stupid, like baseball stats or the bad graffiti on the Art Department door.

My bread stick is tipped slightly but propped up between the two fruits. Like my cock. "Oh, geez." Quickly, I move the stick to the other side of the plate. I peel one of the oranges, doing my best to ignore the heat creeping up *my* neck.

Sammie laughs and sits back in her chair. "I'm sorry. Can't help but give the new kid a hard time."

She still looks uncomfortable but not as much as before, and I relax some. But the "kid" reference annoys me. I yank the rind off the orange and drop it on my tray. "I'm not that young."

Chewing, she sets down her fork and her fingers cover her mouth. "That's not what I meant." But embarrassment returns, like I pulled up some memory she doesn't like.

What am I up against, here? The phantoms in women's heads are more terrifying than any real bad guy. They lunge at you out of nowhere and rip to shreds the world you've built. Like what Dan's ex-wife did to his life.

I must be frowning because now she looks worried. "Believe me, no one looks at you and thinks 'kid.' You're..." She waves her hand at me.

"A moose?" Dan started calling me "moose" when I put on twenty-five pounds during my sophomore year. Wasn't even lifting that much, other than helping at his work.

Sammie laughs and shakes her head. "You *are* big."

I shift in my chair, trying to keep my semi-hard state as comfortable as possible, and our knees bump.

She jumps, startled, and glances under the table. "And long legged."

The front of her shirt opens enough for me to see the edges of her little lacey bra. It's indigo, like her skirt. Her bra matches her *touch me* skirt.

I almost blurt out a dinner invitation. Hell, I almost knock aside the table and take her right here on the floor of the cafeteria.

But Sammie's phone chirps. She pulls it out of her bag and, holding it out, she narrows her eyes as she reads the text. "Damn."

She's not happy. Or she is happy. I can't tell.

"Rick got a second shoot. He's staying in L.A. for an extra few days." Her shoulders tighten, as do her fingers around the phone. She's sitting uncomfortably, the way I would paint her if I wanted to convey anxiety.

My stomach drops and all of a sudden I don't want to eat anymore. This Rick is the reason she's been standoffish.

He causes her discomfort and it leaves a bad taste in my mouth.

He shouldn't treat her that way, I think. Except I don't know what *that way* is. Maybe he never does the dishes. Maybe he leaves his underwear on the floor. Or maybe he doesn't touch her the way she likes.

She looks up from her phone. "You're awfully quiet."

She's right—I haven't said anything for a couple of minutes. Thing is, I don't know what to say. Everything swimming around in my head sounds idiotic. I want to pick her up and set her on my lap and stroke her back instead.

I don't like seeing her upset.

I blink. We've had one lunch and a fair amount of staring and this guy is raising my hackles? Did I learn nothing from Dan's divorce?

Sammie leans forward, her face unreadable, poised to put down her phone. But it chirps again and she stops, looking at the screen with the same narrow eyes as before. Until they widen.

Her entire body stiffens.

"What?" I ask. Probably not what she wants to hear.

Sammie turns the phone around, holding it out. I gently touch her fingers as I take it, knowing I shouldn't be thinking about her skin right now. Whatever is on the phone has her upset.

I look down at the screen. *What time pick you up?* the text reads. *Have exactly what you need. Don't worry baby*.

It's from her asshole boyfriend. I know immediately it wasn't meant for her. So does she. And I know immediately what it means.

"It's vague, right? Maybe he's talking about a script or something." She looks more shocked than anything else.

The phone is still in my hand. "Don't answer it." My head is spinning with options: Wait and see if he realizes who he texted. Wait for his excuse. But what I want to do is type out *Sammie's new boyfriend here. Fuck off.*

I hand back the phone before my thumb gets me in trouble.

She drops it into her bag without looking at it again.

"You alright?" I want to reach across the table and take her hand.

"Why did you say to not answer?" Her face looks blank. She's dropped her hands to her lap like some school girl.

"Let him explain without prompting." I sit back. *Let him dig his own hole.*

Her eyebrows bunch together and she frowns. "Why?"

I look away. *Damn it*, I think, *my chances with her just imploded.* Showing up in the middle of messes like this only leads to problems. "My brother went through a bad divorce a couple years ago. Best thing is to let stuff like that spin itself out without interference." *You get better evidence of infidelity.*

"Oh." Sammie sits for a moment, staring at her half-eaten lunch.

Now my phone beeps. "Shit." I hold it out so Sammie sees my calendar reminder. "I have a meeting in ten."

She nods and drops her napkin on her picked-at lunch. I don't like that she's not eating. It means she's more upset than she's letting on.

"If you need to talk, text me. Okay?" I pile my dishes on the center of my tray. I don't stand and I won't either, until I know she's okay. If I'm late for the meeting, so be it.

Sammie watches me and her face is impassive again. But she nods finally and stands up.

"I'm glad I met you," she says. "Thank you."

If we were alone, or in a restaurant, or outside, or—damn it, I don't know. Anyplace but here. Anyplace other than the cafeteria where we both work, I would have kissed her. Straight up and over the table, a full kiss right on those beautiful lips.

But I breathe because she doesn't need a scene right now. "You're welcome." I lift my tray as I stand, partly to hide my hopefully not that obvious desire to be near her. "Text me." *Or call.*

We walk up to our respective floors and I wait by the Art Department door as she ascends to her level. The indigo skirt hugs lovely hips as she steps one leg up, then the other.

I know one thing for sure: That asshole boyfriend doesn't deserve what he's got.

CHAPTER 5

Samantha

I made it through my embarrassment and ate lunch with Tom. Yes, I can act like an adult. But then he had to go and be perfect. Eight months and Rick has never cared if I'm *okay*. He brought me tea when I had the flu but mostly he stayed back, saying he didn't want to catch my bugs. He never makes sure I'm *okay* okay. He's never even asked me to text when he's gone.

And I doubt his last text was meant for me.

This time, when I open the door to the loft, I don't hit his bike. I hit nothing.

Mickles rubs against my leg, meowing for his dinner. I pick him up, cradling him in my arm, and he headbutts my shoulder as I drop my bag on the floor.

He's soft and smooth under my fingers, a sweet vibrating ball of fluff and love. I breathe, listening to his purr, and try to clear my mind. All I need to do is open the windows. And let in the light.

Part of me thinks I should be ecstatic. My wanting to move out is Rick's fault. All the rolled eyes and the ignoring weren't just his crabby moods. It's always been Rick's fault and I've been picking up subtle cues. But if that's so, then why do I feel so *empty*?

Something needs fixing and I don't know what.

Mickles's food smells terrible but he likes it. I dig in the freezer, the cold numbing my fingers and the rattling drone of the fridge filling the empty loft—and my head—with a constant buzz. I pull out a random microwave dinner and drop it on the counter. Mickles scarfed his entire bowl and now sits in the center of the kitchen floor, cleaning his face.

The cat knows what he wants.

My dinner tastes like paste. I push it away, wishing I'd eaten more of my lunch. An orange right now would taste good.

Some orange on the walls would brighten the entire loft. A little paint, maybe some laughter.

An orange held by one Mr. Tom, Thomas Quidell, peeled slowly and with great care, the way his fingers would peel away my blouse.

Or how I fantasize he'd treat me—gentle pressure along the tight muscles of my neck, strong hands cupping my breasts, his warm, masculine breath teasing my neck.

What am I doing? I think. I pick up my phone. Rick's freaky text is still there, still vague and still weird. I stare at it, thinking it's as strangely lifeless as his loft and I wonder what attracted me to him in the first place.

But I know: I like sex. I like men with hard muscles and strong jaws who like sex, too.

And once again, I wonder why I feel empty.

I absently flick through my contacts. Maybe right now I need a friend more than I need a hot guy. Or maybe a hot guy friend who understands where I'm coming from.

Except my finger brushes past Andy's number. It brushes by all my girlfriends, too. And stops on a place I wasn't expecting: Tom.

Damn it, I think. *Why does he have to be so perfect?* And then I stop thinking. My impulses take over.

I tap away: *Thank you again for lunch.*

A second passes and I drop onto the squeaky couch, staring at what I just did. He said *text me* and I did like some horny kid.

A response pops up: *You are welcome.*

Now what do I do? Ask him if he'd like to get some dinner? Tell him I want a booty call? Lie back on the pillow and add the new and improved Tom to my favorite fantasy?

I'm so fucked up.

Another message pops up: *You okay?*

He didn't type *I'm coming over.* That's what Rick did, the first night we met. I left the party and an hour later I had my ass in the air and a male model pounding away groaning how much he likes chicks who can take what he gives them.

Just a little disoriented, I message back.

Lunch tomorrow.

I stare at my phone. Part of me is screaming *Yes!* while another is screaming *No!* The worst of it is that I don't know why.

Sure. Lunch tomorrow. I set down the phone. Mickles watches me from the back of the couch again, purring like he always does. He drops onto my lap and curls up into a ball of happiness. A cat knows when a moment is good and a cat doesn't care if what's done is bad. Or if what's coming is worse. Cats just know what they like in the moment.

Maybe I should pack my stuff. Or maybe I should wait until Rick is back and we have a moment to talk.

But Rick's not a talker. I don't even know where to start with him.

Never have. Never will.

I stroke Mickles's back, thinking about that space between me and Rick. That big, empty place we often filled with sex because sex is something we can both do. And do well. But when the sun comes up, the curtains are always closed. Nothing gets in.

I lie back on the couch, thinking about how correct I was before: I'm so fucked up.

Thomas

BART'S RUNNING CIRCLES AROUND MY LEGS. "UNCLE TOMMY! UNCLE Tommy!"

I'm not paying him the attention I should because Sammie texted me back: *Lunch tomorrow.*

My brain's yelling *Score!* but I know I shouldn't be smiling like some stupid kid. I need to be careful. Don't need to do dumb shit and end up like Dan.

"Uncle Tommy!" Bart's in his superhero pajamas and he's bouncing on his toes, his arms out, ready to be hoisted into the air.

"Sorry about that, little man." I tuck away the phone and swing him up to my shoulders. "Shouldn't you be in bed?"

He wraps his little hands around my forehead as we bounce along. "Daddy said Uncle Tommy was coming over and that I could stay up so you could tuck me in and then I'll go to sleep because I have school tomorrow and I'm tired." He makes a show of yawning so he can touch the ceiling.

"Well then, we need to do just that."

Dan's leaning against the wall next to the door, grinning. He's set the last of my boxes out for me. With tonight's load, I'm officially out of his basement.

I carry Bart over to his dad and bow so he bops a little on my shoulders. A massive giggle curls from his little boy throat.

"School, huh?" I ask. Bart's four and a year out from kindergarten.

Dan ruffles his son's hair. "Mister Smartypants here got accepted into the Early Childhood Arts program at the center, didn't you?"

Bart bounces on my shoulders. "I did! I did! I told them I want to be a painter like my Uncle Tommy and Ms. Frasier is my teacher and she's really pretty."

"Really pretty, huh?" I look to Dan and he nods *Oh yeah.* I laugh. We're three peas from the same pod, us Quidell men. "Is she a really good teacher?"

"She's got Bart here painting pictures every day, doesn't she?" Dan lifts his son off my shoulders and sets him down.

"Yes!" Bart's pantomiming painting and he squints, holding out his thumb.

Dan laughs and scoots Bart toward the stairs. "Off to brush your teeth. Uncle Tommy will tuck you in when you're done."

Bart stands straight. "I brushed my teeth!"

Dan kneels down, his face exaggerated into an unbelieving smirk. "And when did you do this?"

"Yesterday."

I laugh again, remembering saying the exact same thing to our dad when I was little.

Dan shakes his head and sends Bart off. "Go on." He watches his son climb the stairs and we both listen to the soles of Bart's footie bottoms whiff on the carpet.

"You texting with a woman?" Dan doesn't look at me. He's watching Bart turn on the bathroom light.

"Yes." No use lying about it or acting upset about the question. He's my big brother. "Her name is Sammie. Met her at work."

Dan nods but doesn't say anything more. I know what he's thinking, though: Please be careful. Don't do what I did.

I glance up the stairs. Dan went through hell with his divorce. But at least he got Bart. "Thanks for packing up the last of my stuff."

Dan rolls his eyes. "Why do you keep all those old drawings? There's stuff from high school in there."

High school, college—some people keep a journal. I keep my drawings. "I'm a hoarder. You'll need to commit me in a few months. Start planning now."

Dan chuckles. "You got some hand drawn porn in there." He smirks and kicks at one of the boxes. "That's why you keep it. Admit it."

"If only." But I used to draw every pretty woman I saw. Out on the mall in front of the art building, while sitting on the grass in front of the library—

A memory slaps me hard: My first month on campus, an upperclassman walking by, her lovely auburn hair in a ponytail, her head turning as she watched me watch her.

"Man, you alright?" Dan slaps my shoulder. "You look like you just saw a ghost."

Maybe I did. A ghost I share with Sammie.

And maybe *my* phantom is big enough, strong enough, to wrestle into submission whatever is swirling around in her head.

❧

BACK HOME, I KNEEL IN MY "LIVING ROOM" NEXT TO MY apartment's big sliding glass door. The balcony is three feet deep, just enough for a chair and a pot of tomatoes. It's the reason I took this place. The door lets in brilliant afternoon light.

The room has one chair. My monitors sit on my desk, in the dining area off the little kitchenette. I usually eat on the balcony or at my work table, which sits where a normal person would have a couch.

The place screams bachelor—working bachelor—but it gets the job done. I did spring for a big comfy mattress, the only furniture in the apartment's one bedroom.

Inside the box of old drawings, I find some comic book-inspired work from middle school, a couple still lifes from high school, and my target: one of my small drawing pads from my freshman year of college.

The memories rush back in: The play of light on the grass I favored. The laughter and the sounds of bikes rushing by. The smell of coffee and fast food.

Some of the pages are smudged. Some not. I flip through the book, searching.

And there she is, walking by, her lush hair in a ponytail and her backpack riding high on her back. She'd glanced over her shoulder, watching me more than where she was walking, and I had to draw her. I had to capture that face.

Sammie, four years ago, just as she was graduating. We'd had a moment. Too brief and never followed up, but it happened. And I had proof.

I stare at the drawing for a long second. I'd used pencil for this one. It had faded some around her shoulders, but her face lifts off of the paper, beautiful and perfect. Somehow, I'd managed to get it right.

I'll give it to her tomorrow. Even if nothing comes of it, she needs to know not all men see her the way her boyfriend does. Some men see what's truly there.

That asshole is going to lose her, if it's the last thing I do.

CHAPTER 6

Samantha

We're outside today, sitting at the picnic table under the sad maple tree in the tiny municipal park next to our building. There's an ugly piece of seventies public art at the intersection of the two sidewalks bisecting the lawn, and the tree shades it as much as the picnic table.

But we take what we can get. This is one of the few open grassy areas in the entire downtown that hasn't been turned into a parking lot and there are always employees out here, taking in a bit of sun.

Tom is telling me about his family and I'm chewing my sandwich. We're eating the same thing for lunch again today, but I'm pretty sure he chose the same I did on purpose this time because he keeps making a face when he bites into his Reuben. I didn't think anything could make him more handsome, but the frowny-face does.

His eyes light up when he talks about his nephew and his gestures become more animated when he tells me how Bart likes to draw just like his Uncle Tommy. When he shows me Bart's picture I can't help but smile. I'm watching Tom, listening, thinking he's not only unbelievably hot, but also a good person. And interesting.

"You have two brothers?" Two other Quidell men walk the world, probably both just as flawless as Tom.

He nods. "Dan used to be a firefighter, until his injury. Now he has his own company." A new frown works across his face as he takes a bite of his lunch, chews, and swallows it down. "Rob starts grad school next year. Cultural Anthropology."

Smart, too. But I could have guessed that.

We're quiet for a moment, both finishing our sandwiches. After we'd ordered he'd tucked his hand around my back and ushered me through the crowd using his big shoulders to clear a path.

I don't know why, but it made me feel special.

"Rick's coming home tomorrow night." I blurt it out. I never blurt. I think I need some insight, some support on this, and for some reason, my instincts tell me to talk to Tom about it, and not Andy. Maybe because Andy's always had a crush on Rick.

Tom sits back. He watches me with his intense blue-green eyes, and his jaw hardens. He truly is a big guy; he's wide enough to block all the glare bouncing off the public art behind him.

"What are you going to do?" He wants to cross his arms but he doesn't—I can see his shoulders twitch like he's fighting it.

Move out and spend the rest of my life subduing my sex drive by masturbating to my old fantasy of your former self? I think.

A blush creeps up my neck and I look away. I've been doing pretty well on keeping control of the color creeping up my neck. I don't want to lose a friend because I can't keep my hormones in check. "I'm thinking I should move out." I can't read his response. He's holding his body perfectly still and with the bright light out here it's difficult to read the subtle twitches of his face.

"Do you have a place to stay?" He says it slow and I can tell he's watching me carefully.

"I don't know. I haven't asked anyone." Sitting straight, I look around. I could ask Andy, but I haven't seen him all week. This isn't something to text someone about. "My family is in Grand Forks. Finding a new apartment first would probably be the best idea."

His phone beeps. "Shit. Listen, I have another meeting." Stuffing it back in his pocket, he stands up. "I think I need to work on scheduling, huh?"

He's smiling and I feel better. The wonderful person in front of me is willing to go through the hell of rescheduling meetings in our meeting-heavy workplace just so he can spend longer lunches with me.

I don't think I've ever had lunch with Rick. When he comes downtown, he's always too busy.

"Drinks after work?" Tom touches my elbow but pulls his hand back like he's afraid he did something bad.

I don't think Rick ever touches my arms, either, except to hold me down.

"Okay," I say. Drinks with a friend is, I think, what I need right now.

"We'll get this worked out. You don't have to live somewhere you don't want to." Tom takes both trays and waits as I stand and loop my bag over my arm. The shadow he throws is almost as big as the one cast by the art, and for a second I wonder if I should be intimidated. I'm not. But his presence offers a comfort I'm not used to.

As I stand in this little park surrounded by coworkers chatting on their phones and the constant downtown traffic noise, I wonder why I've been fighting moving out. Because I have.

Why do I keep going back to the loft? For a split second, I wonder if it's as simple—and as pathetic—as not wanting to be alone.

But I don't think so.

I smile. "After work it is. I'll come down and meet you. Okay?"

Tom smiles too, a big grin like I'd expect to see on this little nephew's face when the kid wants to share a secret but can't because he *promised*.

"Okay, what's up?" I throw him an exaggerated look of suspicion just to see what he'll do. He doesn't disappoint.

The grin turns into a big, full-body wiggle of happiness. When a man does the quick body dance of excitement—not a kid, but a gorgeous guy—it's like every glacier on the planet has melted and everything's blooming. He's not just a big dude capable of scary things, but a full person with joy in his heart.

"I have something for you." He's still grinning, and still just as gorgeous.

"Oh my God you didn't buy me a car, did you?" I'm sure I'm smiling just as much because there's no way I couldn't be, even though I'm joking.

A wonderful, hearty laugh rolls out of Tom. "Been on the job three weeks, my lovely, beautiful Sammie. A new car won't be coming for at least six months." Tom ushers me back toward the door, winking.

He said *lovely, beautiful Sammie*. He stacks the trays and lays his hand on my back, at waist level the same way he did when we came outside.

But this time I feel the strength of his fingers. This time, I want more than just his forearm rubbing my skin through my blouse. I want to be against his side, feeling those arms wrap around all of me. I want to be close enough to smell his subtle-but-rich scent. To breathe in masculinity and consideration and art.

He's juggling the trays and lifts his hand off my back, his attention completely on the tip weight of what he's holding and not at all on what's playing over my face. And I'm glad, because if he did see, I'd be embarrassed beyond anything I felt when I realized *he* was my fantasy freshman.

Much more embarrassed.

Which I shouldn't be. Or maybe I should. I walk alongside Mr. Tom Quidell, chatting small talk. He won't tell me what he has for me. And I don't say anything about wanting right now, more than anything else in the world, to kiss him.

And the embarrassment just grows.

When we walk the stairs to our floors, he smiles again and watches my face like he can't quite figure out what he's seeing. "Drinks in four hours. No backing out." He gives me a mock stern look.

I must be hiding my embarrassment well, so I grin and wag my finger at him. "You said you have something for me. I want it."

Tom laughs as he opens the graffiti door. "Off to your dungeon my queen, before the knaves find us missing from our tortures." He bows and vanishes from the stairwell, hurrying off to his meeting.

Ahead, I have four hours of stewing in the emotions rolling around inside my body. Four hours of a clenched gut that can't decide if it wants to force me to run and hide or jump for joy.

I stare at the door thinking, once again, the one thought that's been blinking in my mind for the past few days like a giant neon light: I'm so fucked up.

But this time it's dancing with another thought: I know how much Rick likes the "fucked up" me. I think, for him, it's useful. It's that bit of distance that allows him to do whatever the hell he wants.

I never hid it from Rick. We never talked about it, either. I suppose it's not fair to hide it from Tom. So the question is, how much "fucked up" will Tom tolerate?

CHAPTER 7

Thomas

The bar across the street from our building serves a good selection of beers, but Sammie sits across from me in the dim booth with a glass of malbec in front of her. She leans forward, playing with her napkin, and for a second I get a good look at her cleavage.

I want to crawl over the dark table top to the deep red leather of her side of the booth and pull her into the corner. I want to kiss that frown right off her face while I rub my palm across her exceptional breasts.

And maybe get her to look at me.

She's been avoiding eye contact since we came in. We chatted about work and weekend plans, because it's Friday. All it did was remind her that her asshole boyfriend would be home tomorrow evening.

Now she's on her second glass of wine. She hasn't eaten anything, either. So I'm wondering. "You going to be okay on your bus trip home?" She's not that big, though she is taller than most women. To me, she's the perfect size.

She looks up this time, meeting my gaze, and sighs. "What do you have for me?"

I shake my head. "It's in my truck. And don't change the subject."

She sits up. "In your truck, huh?"

I can't tell what she's thinking but her body looks tentative. "When we leave, I'll get it."

Quiet, she watches me. After another sip, she sits back. "You're too perfect, do you know that?"

I almost spit my beer across the table. It's not that good anyway—it's bitter—and I set it down instead. "I'm too perfect?" *God damn*, I think. Is she flirting with me? It's dark in here and a shadow fell across her face when she sat back. Could I be lucky enough to have her *flirt* with me?

"You're right. I don't need to live someplace I don't want to." Her delicate hand lifts her glass off the table and it disappears into the shadow as she sips. "I think I should have had something to eat."

"We can get something. Or go down the street to the new Thai place." *Or I can drive you home*, I think. Drive her to her door, go in with her, and pack up all her possessions and take her back to my place.

"At least I have my work shit together." She shrugs and sips again. "And you, to make sure I'm not a hazard to my fellow bus passengers."

Her gaze flits to my face as if she's waiting for me to run away. But I know what she's doing. She's laying out her insecurities because every woman knows nothing chases off a man faster than showing "senseless vulnerability." Or at least that's what Dan says.

I'd rather see her demons now, though, and not three years into a marriage, thank you very much.

I blink, watching her, and my chest tightens. Thinking about Sammie and *three years into a marriage* at the same time is, in all honesty, much scarier than any of her self-doubts.

"You know why Rick likes me?" She sniffs and swirls what's left of her wine. Then she thrusts out her breasts.

I almost spit out my beer again. "That can't be the *only* reason."

She opens her mouth like she's about to spill every detail of their sex life but snaps it shut. Her jaw clenches.

It *is* the only reason he likes her. What kind of asshole is this guy?

She waves her hand in the air. "It's my fault. It's the only reason I like him."

I don't know what to say. Living with someone just for the sex would be fun, I suppose. For a while.

"Why do you do that to yourself?" It's the only question my brain musters.

Across from me, Sammie steels herself. She's going to give me an honest answer and I know from the way she's looking at me that this is a test. I know it the way I know she's unbelievably beautiful. I may not be able to read women's faces, but this body language screams louder than Bart when he wants a new video game.

"I like sex," she says. She's owning it, not flinching or backing down and goddamn, it makes her hotter. I want to rub my face between her breasts. And my cock.

"That doesn't explain why you're living with him." I own it too—if she's testing me by showing what she considers her warts, then I'll give her honest answers. I won't be chased off by my own discomfort.

"No, it doesn't." She takes another sip.

My napkin bunches up under my fingers. "It seems like you're ashamed."

She doesn't look at me. "Why would I be ashamed?"

That's just it. I don't know why she would be ashamed. She's lovely and fun and if she needs to own anything in her life, it's that. "You can like sex. You don't need to separate it from the rest of your life. Well, maybe work." I grin, trying to ease some of her tension. Though backing her against the wall under the stairs would be a nice distraction between meetings.

Sammie grins back at me and taps her temple. "I grew up in the suburbs of a small city. Maybe I have stuff in my head I don't know about."

"Don't we all?" Blaming her ghosts wouldn't change anything, though.

"I'm frustrated when I can't have the sex I want." She takes another sip. "Rick's been tired lately. Says he's been training too hard and he'd rather sleep."

Whoa, I think. I suspect my eyes got big. "No *fucking* way." He's denying Sammie? Who the hell would deny Sammie? My hand slaps the table top. "I'd rather be close to my woman than train, or play video games, or drink, or anything else. A weight bench is no one's muse."

Her face changes. Her cheeks soften and her eyes grow big. Just for a second.

I wonder if I just passed the test.

"You have a much healthier view of sex than I do."

I laugh. "If you think abstinence is healthy." I roll my eyes.

"What?" Now she looks equal parts shocked and confused.

I laugh again. "Been living in my brother's basement, remember? Makes a man bad dating material."

"Oh my God. I can't believe I'm talking to you about this. You must think I'm a crazy person." She downs her wine, a new embarrassment creeping up her neck, and glances at her watch. "Who is about to miss her bus."

My hand wraps around her wrist before she can stand up. "I'll drive you home. Besides, I have something for you, remember?"

"Oh..." She's staring at me and her eyes are huge. Really huge.

"Sammie, you're not crazy."

"But I am fucked up," she whispers.

Ah, the ever-present ghost haunting a lot of women. I wrap my fingers around her hand, holding gently. She looks down at our clasped fingers, our touching palms, and sighs again.

"My brother's ex was fucked up. You are not fucked up. You just need to figure out a few things."

She nods, still looking at our hands. "Will you drive me home?"

"Of course." I'll do more than drive her home. I'll do everything I can for her.

CHAPTER 8

Samantha

Tom digs around behind the seat of his clean-but-older truck. It's flame red and looks like it's had work done to it and I wonder if it's an old firefighter's vehicle.

I stare at his ass. It's magnificently framed by his black slacks and I can't help myself. I'd be staring at it even if I hadn't drunk two glasses of wine on an empty stomach and had a frank talk with him about sex.

Sometimes my mouth just blabs.

"Ah!" Tom pulls his head out and stands up tall, a cardboard tube in his hand. "Here it is." He hands me the tube.

It looks just like the one he handed me at the beginning of the week, when we first met, and for a second I wonder if it's more mock-ups.

He must have read my mind because he chuckles. "No logos. I promise."

I pop off the top. Inside, there's a single rolled up sheet of paper and I finger it carefully, making sure I don't damage it.

It unrolls as I pull it out.

I'm looking at myself. Me, with a backpack over my shoulders and my hair longer, and in a ponytail. Like I used to wear it, when I was still at the University.

That day, the day of my fantasy, when I was looking at him, he was looking at me. And he drew a picture. Of me.

"I found it last night." He's grinning like a kid again, and his happiness reasserts itself when he points at the drawing. "I did this my first semester. It's you. I'm positive."

It's stunning. The emotions he captured sing off the paper: I'm tentative and unsure. There's desire in my eyes, but it's not to be. And there's a sadness to the lines, as if he, too, wanted a connection, but also decided it wasn't to be.

"I don't know what to say." In my hands right now is a real, physical manifestation of what, for me all these past four years, had been nothing but a dream. A desire I could never make real. "This is beyond beautiful."

For a moment, long ago, I had been Tom's muse.

"I'd like to draw a new one."

I look up at his handsome face and his tousled hair. He still wants me to be his muse? Even after I did my damnedest to scare him off?

My answer popped out of my mouth before all the embarrassment —all the fucked-up-edness—can cut it off. "When?" Not *Why?* or *Really?* I ask *when.*

Somewhere in my brain, I understand what I want. Damn it, I need to own it.

Something about his stance changes. He feels closer all of a sudden, as if we're touching. Like I just passed a test for him.

Because I want this. I want to be his muse. I want to give to him across all his senses.

Hunger overtakes his face and his eyes darken for a moment. When he speaks, his voice is low and deep. "Now."

"Now?"

Tom nods. He's got a look of determination about him and I realize this is as much about him not letting me run off to my loft-cave as it is about wanting to draw my picture.

Maybe more.

"But it's night."

"Candles, then."

"Right now?" Why am I waffling? I want this. But maybe I don't deserve it.

Tom takes my hand, his grip firm but polite, and my body responds before I can think. Again. I'm tingling. Up my arm from where he holds my fingers. Down my belly to between my legs. Into my neck and up across the back of my mouth.

I suck in my breath and my breasts thrust out. My lip curls in and I bite down.

He pulls me around his truck and opens the passenger side. "Up you go. We'll get take-out and you will eat low mein out of a box while you sit for me in the candlelight."

My heel slips on the running board but Tom has me. He keeps me from falling, his hand on my ass.

He's cupping my backside, his fingers splayed, like he knows how to give me the right kind of spanking. I must have shivered because he let go.

"Buckle in, my lovely Sammie," he purrs, the wonder of his baritone flowing over me. When I settle in, he's walking around the front of the truck, but his eyes are on me.

I feel like I'm on that desk in the library, the one in my fantasy. But this time, it's twenty-three-year-old Tom bending over me with his breath tickling my nipples and his palm rubbing me just so.

When he gets into the truck, he slams the door and I jolt back into the here and now. *Shit*, I think. *I'm going to fuck him tonight*. It's going to happen.

I want to crawl onto his lap as much as I want to run away.

"You will be my first guest." He starts the truck but he's looking at me with his gorgeous eyes and I can't read his face.

How is this going to help me feel less fucked up? A sane woman would say next weekend, let me move out first.

But I'd waffle about that, too. Why, I don't know. It's not Rick I want anymore.

CHAPTER 9

Thomas

S ammie stands in the center of my living room, her back to me and her smooth little ass tight and her heels together like she's trying to keep her pussy clenched. Fucking her right now, on the floor between my easel and balcony door, would be as easy as taking those five strides across the room. But I walk into the kitchen instead, though the walking is uncomfortable, and drop dinner on the counter.

I can wait. I *will* wait. She's not going to leave here thinking I'm no different from her dumbass soon-to-be ex-boyfriend.

"Your curtains are open." She says it in a dreamy voice, as if seeing the outside world makes her happy.

I dig around for forks. I have to do something to distract myself. Damn, she's beautiful. "I like the sun." Glancing over, I see the last of the sunset play along the lines of her body. She's silhouetted in golds and reds, her black and gray patterned skirt curving around her hips and her hand, holding a bottle of water, at her side.

Her lovely hair is up in a loose ponytail. Little wisps frame the line of her perfect jaw when she looks over her shoulder. "I like it, too."

No more of that boyfriend. She makes a decision tonight. Then I clean out her stuff from that apartment. If I need to take her to her friend Andy's, so be it. But she deserves better than what she's letting herself have.

"Is the floor okay?" I point at my work table and shrug. Six or seven drawings lay scattered over the top and I don't want to move them. "I have a system."

Sammie laughs, pulled, it seems, from her dreaminess. "Men with systems are always better."

I didn't think I'd want her to stay more than I do right now, but I can't let her go. Not without a good reason. I hand her a box of takeout.

She stares at it for a second. Winking, she pulls off her heels and drops to the floor, both her legs off to one side so she can sit like a lady. Patting the floor, she reaches for me.

Me. Not the food. My hand.

I almost drop the food and roll on top of her. Almost rip open her blouse and lay kisses over her chest while growling some vague words declaring my possession. Because for a flittering moment, those primal needs surface above my civilized caution and the lower parts of my brain—and the lower part of my body—all scream *my woman*.

Jealousy flicks into my vision and for a split second I see some manscaped douchebag model-boy pawing at her chest and forcing her down on him.

I blink. I'm still standing, still holding the low mein. She's looking me up and down—at my face and my chest and my crotch. My boxer-briefs can only keep my cock under so much control.

I grin sheepishly and drop down next to her, handing over her meal. She takes it, looking away again, over her shoulder and out the window. "You don't seem like a candles kind of guy."

Her skirt hikes an inch or two up her legs when she sets down her food. The top of one thigh-high stocking peeks out.

She says something. "What?" I ask.

Her gaze moves from the moon to the easel. "You said candlelight. Will you be able to see well enough to draw?"

The sun's gone and the full glory of the evening moon scatters across her hand. She dances her fingers across the carpet. Rustling drifts in from outside—the wind has picked up. A cloud rolls through the sky and for a second my living room drops into shadow.

I don't say anything. I stand instead and she watches me as I rise, her lovely face turning up. She looks hungry, but not for the food next to her. She looks like she wants to escape.

I need to capture her state on paper. I need for her to understand that I see it when I look at her, and that I'm here for her. She has a choice.

"Don't move," I say. She blinks, but follows my command, staying perfectly still as I walk to the linen closet in the hallway. Dan sent a box of pillar candles, old ones his ex left. I think he wanted them out of his house.

A couple are sweet smelling. A few, spicy. One smells like vanilla and I pull it out when I set the candles down next to my work table.

Sammie watches me, her hand still splayed in the moonbeam, her face in shadow. Bending down and kissing her would be the easiest thing in the world. Tasting those perfect lips. Flicking my tongue against hers. But I back away toward the kitchen for a lighter and plates for the candles.

The apartment drops into twilight when I turn off the kitchen light. Only the silver glow of the moon frames Sammie where she sits on the floor, her long legs to the side. I set a candle next to the easel. The lighter bursts on, a little sun in our night, and the candle sputters alive. A new glow brightens Sammie from the front, a warm wash of light and vanilla.

"It smells nice." She sits up a little, obviously uncomfortable leaning to the side because of her skirt.

I pull two pillows and a throw off my chair. Leaning toward her, I catch the tiny hint of wine still left on her breath. But mostly I hear the small hitch in her breath and the whiffing of her blouse's fabric against her bra.

The first pillow I tuck under her arm. The second, behind her back. The throw, I bunch up under her hip.

"Thank you," she whispers, and lays down, rolling against the pillow behind her and stretching out along the throw on the floor. Her breasts thrust up. She sighs softly, her eyes closing for a second, then reopening to look up at the moon now dappling her face.

Her fingers wiggle. Her hips sway. And I swear she's having a tiny orgasm right now, right in front of me.

I want to rub against her. I want to pull those legs apart and nip her skin along the top of those stockings. I want to pump into her fast and hard and make her come more times in one night than that dick ex of hers has the entire time they've been together.

But it's not my choice when he becomes her ex. It's hers. And she might tease—consciously or not, I'm not sure—but she's going to say it to me. She's going to tell me explicitly what she wants.

And she's going to want me.

"Take out the ponytail." I'm growling. I swear to God I sound like some animal. When I get between those thighs I will be an animal.

She lifts her head and a small wicked smile curls up her lips, but she doesn't say a word. Her fingers smooth up her side and pull free her hair. It cascades over her shoulders, over the throw, and into the moonbeam. When she lays her head down again, her fingers stay next to her lips.

"You are killing me." It comes out even deeper than before. I can barely talk. But I somehow manage to pull my pad down from the easel and my pastels from my case.

The moon casts silver from behind and the candle golden orange from the front. She's bathed in contradiction and I need to capture it as much as I need to capture her. The candlelight flickers over her skin, over her flimsy blouse, and I see the outline of her bra underneath as it curves around her full breasts. Her nipples must be hard little nubs under it, but I can't see.

If I ran my hand over each breast, first the left, then the right, squeezing, I'd find those rock hard nipples. Flick them each with my tongue. Make her scream my name.

I drop onto the floor and prop the pad against the easel's leg. Sammie watches me, calm and almost dozing. We don't speak.

I draw.

CHAPTER 10

Samantha

Tom settles into brilliant intensity and I'm hypnotized. He sits three feet away behind his paper but I feel his gaze on me, assessing, reading, wanting. He moves his hands to draw an arc and I feel his fingertips on my skin. My need for him lifts away with his artist's touch, but it doesn't leave. It floats above my hip like a ghost waiting to be given permission.

He tilts his head and my frozen soul lifts up as well. I feel the ice that's been locking me into one place hover now just outside my mind. Like it's a separate thing that's been too close for me to see. But Tom draws a line, makes a sweep of color, and pulls it to his paper, giving the phantom a visible shape.

I've been, I think, a mirror to Rick, reflecting back his physical attraction to himself. He banks it, lives it, sells it, but it's flat and thin.

But when Tom watches me, I can tell he sees the dimensions he wants to lay down on his page—and, from the brilliant hard-on outlined in his pants, to touch. He's not flat. Or thin. And I want, more than anything right now, to get rid of my phantoms. To let in this living man.

Slowly, carefully, I unbutton my blouse. If Tom is willing to look beyond my surface to find what's below the mirror, I'll show him. I'll open up.

I hear his pastels scrape across the paper. The candle flickers and the scent of vanilla fills the air, and Tom's gaze wraps his strong will around my body. Tom yanks away the sheen I've been using since college to reflect back to the men I want to bed what they want to see.

Somehow, it became my cover. I could have as much sex as my body wanted but I never showed my partners *me*. Mostly, they didn't want to see me, anyway. They just wanted their cocks sucked.

But Tom wants me. He wants to see. I don't think he wants a relationship with someone who hides from him, and with each fill of gold or blue on his paper he's demanding I tell him the truth.

His hand stops for a moment as he watches me undo my blouse, but he doesn't set down his work.

I know why. He's not seeing me yet. That mirror is still there, and I'm still behind it. I feel it, drifting over my skin. It's cold, frosty. And I need to shed it.

Slowly, I arch my back and slip off the blouse. A groan rolls from his throat, a deeply male vibration. His fingers set down the pastel and without looking at his paper he flips it over to a fresh page.

He's taking in the curve of my back and the line of my legs. His gaze stops at my hip and he tilts his head again, his eyes piercing, but he doesn't ask me to take off my skirt. He only watches.

I unhook the button and undo the zipper, easing the fabric down my legs. It rubs against my stockings, sounding much like his charcoal against the page.

I want him against me. I want to see the hard muscles of his thighs. To feel the v of his abs. I want to know if he keeps his chest smooth or if I'll rub my face against hair. Will he whisper when we make love? Will he make the small sounds that drive me crazy?

He's beautiful, my Tom. He sits, one leg propped up, leaning toward his paper, a charcoal in his hand. A smudge marks his cheek where he rubbed his face. I want to lick it, to feel with my tongue what this wonderful man does with his hands.

I smell the hot scent of the candle and its flickering heat, but it's

Tom's focus that reddens my skin. He holds me without touching even as I release the skirt from around my hips. The tops of my stockings grip my thighs and I'm suddenly very aware of their tight hold.

It should be Tom holding my thighs. Tom widening my legs. Tom staring down with all the intensity I see in his eyes right now.

I could crawl across the floor. Pinch the zipper of his trousers between my thumb and finger and release what's waiting for me. How smooth is he? Is he velvet, like in my fantasy? Is he thick and hard enough to make me scream? Will I swirl my tongue around the head of his cock and hear his groans?

Can I make him crazy enough to thrust into my mouth even though he's a gentleman?

"Sammie."

I blink, pulled from my revelry, and I realize my hand is between my thighs. I'm stroking myself, thinking about the gorgeous man in front of me. About his beautiful eyes and his wonderful hair I want to tangle my fingers into. About his chest and arms, so large they cover me completely. About his dexterous fingers and the joy they promise.

My mind knows what's possible and my fingers are determined to give me a touch, a taste.

"Sammie, look at me."

The candle's light flickers over his arm, his shoulders. His white dress shirt—his work shirt—glows. The leather cord around his neck stands out as a deep line. I want to lick it, to take it away. Nothing should mar this man's skin.

He sets the pad against the easel without turning it. I can't see what he's drawn and I think he wants it that way. For now.

"Talk to me." Tom wipes his smudged fingers on a cloth from the easel.

No words have passed between us for so long I feel mute. The moon's silver slices across my bare shoulder, into the glow of the candle, and I shiver. I'm stuck between two places—between the cold out there and the warm hardness in here.

"Tell me what you're thinking. Please." He's still rock hard. All this time he's been drawing me and I've been stripping for him, he's been straining the seams of his trousers. He hasn't touched. Hasn't slipped his fingers into the cup of my bra and plied my breasts, his hot breath on my neck.

"You haven't touched me." I'm spread before him with only the deep red lace of my bra and panties between me and his strong hands. Between me and his cock.

"You haven't touched *me*, Sammie." He's next to me now, so close I feel the heat rising off his skin, but he keeps his hands away. "God, you are beautiful."

I want to know this man, to be tasted by him, to feel his tongue and his lips against my mouth, my nipples, my clit. The fantasy won't work anymore. I need the real Tom.

I reach to unbutton his shirt but he stops me, his hand wrapping my wrist and holding me firm.

"You have no idea how much I want you." Tom's voice fills the room, a booming, low call that plays up my spine.

His words resonate inside my head and chest, flooding between my legs. He has no idea how much I want *him*. The need flickering in my belly is like an animal. It wants out. It wants Tom *in*, his cock gliding in and out on my slickness.

"Then let me touch," I whisper. "Let me suck you." Let me feel.

His eyes narrow for a split second. He releases my wrist but leans away toward his easel. Chest out, body elongated, for a moment Tom is on his back and the full wonder of the bulge in his pants is plain to see.

I groan, staring, wanting nothing more than to touch. I need to know. My fingers work his belt.

But he sits up again before I undo the clasp. "Wait."

He has the cloth in his hands. The one with the smudges he used to clean his fingers. He folds it over and over until it's a clean, white, long rectangle and all evidence of his work is on the inside.

I watch the cloth. Other men have tried to tie me up. I don't like it. Why, I don't know, but it's not my thing.

His face crunches up in frustration. "I want you to feel the difference between what you had and what you could have now." His hand tightens around the fabric. "I'm not him."

"No, you are not." *You are much, much better*, I think. His art, his work, his soul, his body all curl around me. Tom is focused, but he's not Rick. He's not *flat*.

Maybe I can distract him from his cloth. I fumble with his zipper again but he pulls away my hand.

"Sammie, wait."

"I don't want to wait. I can't wait. Not any—"

His mouth covers mine. I lose all my breath to this man—he draws it out of me as if he's sucking out poison. I'm left a blank slate.

No more words circle in my head. That place I go when I hit the fantasy is here, alive. It's his world, his context. It's this room he's filled to the brim with creation, with paints and charcoal and paper. With his weighty easel and the stacks of canvas against the wall. With the lone candle on the floor and the pool of heat it throws. The room lacks the expected bits of life he's supposed to have. Chairs. A couch. But what Tom has is so much better. So much more alive.

He tastes the same as his scent—male and warm. His lips work hungrily over mine and I respond with a greedy need I didn't know I had. This isn't just about wanting to feel his muscles tighten and flex as he fucks me or about knowing he wants it as much as I do. Nor is it about moving on.

His hand finds my breast and he palms my nipple through the cup of my bra, groaning into my mouth, and my back arches in response. Maybe he whispers my name. Maybe he's like me, unable to talk. We both shudder.

His tongue flits into my mouth and tangles with mine. I lose my remaining breath.

Why is he still dressed? I paw at his shirt, pulling and tugging. I need access to his chest. To his skin. I feel his hard muscles under my palms but I can't see. I need to see.

He wraps the cloth from his easel around my eyes.

I stiffen.

"I want you to feel, Sammie," he rumbles, his lips taking my earlobe much the same way they took my mouth. Nibbles flicked my skin, both cold and hot at the same time. My scalp tingles and I sigh, letting him tie the blindfold. "That's all. Just feel."

The world drops into darkness, but Tom is against me, pressing his still covered erection into my belly, and I somehow know where everything is. The candle's heat gives the room directionality. The pillows and throw feel soft against my bare back, the carpet rough. And Tom's clothes rub against the lace of my panties, demanding entrance.

"Tom..." I whisper. He's on top of me, heavy and strong, and his mouth works along my jaw.

His fingers stroke mine, weave into mine, and he pulls my arms up over my head. "Touch me, Sammie." But he lifts away.

Cold air rushes over my breasts and I gasp, wanting him back. How did I live before, without his body on mine? Why, four years ago, did I pass this up?

I reach for him, my hands grasping, though I can't see. But I know where he is. I know he's kneeling between my legs, my magnificent Tom, waiting.

I won't disappoint him.

CHAPTER 11

Samantha

Sitting up, my fingers find his hips. I glide them along his belt, feeling a hitch with each loop. His zipper feels hot, the metal teeth vicious, and I need to release him from his torture. He's rubbing against my hand like he can't help himself and a rush of power rolls through my body. He blindfolded me, but not to dominate, and I understand what he meant by *I want you to feel*.

First, my hands pull his shirt out of his waistband. The fabric crinkles in my grip, crisp as a white dress shirt should be. I find the bottom button and carefully, slowly, undo it.

A low groan rolls from Tom. I imagine him looking down, his face intense. His eyes are full of carnal joy because he's watching me—blindfolded me in only my bra and panties—and I trace my fingers over his abdomen as I undo the next button.

But I don't *know* what he's experiencing. "What do you see right now?" I have to know. I undo another button.

The shirt twists and his hand touches my shoulder, my cheek. "What I want."

I'd been a mirror, I think, to protect myself. Maybe also to hide.

But I can't now. Touching forces me out from behind my glass wall and I whisper his name. "Tom."

"Sammie." His hand curls into my hair and his stomach suddenly pulls away from me. A kiss takes my mouth, hot and intense. Once again, he pulls the poison from my body.

I pull away and he groans, his hands finding my breasts. He's pinching, rubbing and the fabric constrains. I wiggle, reaching for the hooks, but his fingers find them first. My bra lets go.

A vibration moves through his torso as if he's let out a subsonic growl, and his mouth descends to my chest. No man has responded to seeing and sucking at my breasts with so much masculine joy. I almost burst apart, broken into little bits of sensation caused by Tom's roving mouth and possessive hands.

I force his shirt down his arms and he lifts off me. Cold rushes between us and for a split second I don't know where he is, but fabric crinkles—I hear him pull it off—and I orient again. My body knows where Tom is. As does my focus.

Undoing a belt while blindfolded is more difficult than I expected. A giggle pops out and Tom laughs too, until he cups my breasts.

"I want to rub my cock right here." His palm slides between them, over my heart. "I want you to feel it everywhere."

Oh, God, I think. I'm through his belt, through the zipper, to the cotton weave of his boxer-briefs. I have no idea what color they are, but my mind screams *black*. His briefs lie flat over the hard muscles of his hips and I run my hands between his trousers and fabric, feeling the square perfection of his ass. I don't touch his cock. Not yet.

When I pull his hips toward me, I get the full wonder of his hardness against my face. A breathy moan pushes between my lips. My mouth waters—I want to taste him. I *have* to taste him. He releases himself from the boxer-briefs and his cock springs against my lips.

His shaft feels velvety under my fingers, and rock hard. He's long and thick—perfectly shaped. And all I want is to run my tongue over his sensitive head.

I smooth his pre-cum over my lips, tasting him. He's intense, exotic, and I take him into my mouth, working slowly. He wants me to feel, and I want it too. I want this with him, to be aware of his entire body's responses, and not just the force of his cock as it hits the back of my throat.

"Jesus, Sammie." His hips tense under my hands.

I'm taking him deep, swirling my tongue and sucking so hard my cheeks pull in. One hand helping my mouth while the other brushes through his trimmed pubic hair.

I want to see. I feel the v of his hips and the ripple of his abs, and I want to *see*. I lift away my hand to fiddle with the cloth over my eyes.

"Leave it on," he croaks out as he stops my fingers from lifting away the blindfold.

I stop vacuuming his cock, but I keep its perfect head in my mouth, waiting. What else is he going to do? My body screams—I can't take much more. Every inch of my skin ripples as if my nerves are jumping up and down like screaming fanatics. Tom makes every single one of my cells swoon.

His hands grip my breasts again and he pulls them up, making me arch my back. My head falls back and I exhale hard. My entire body moves and the next thing I feel—the next thing I know—is his cock rubbing against first my left nipple, then my right. I want to scream. It feels *good*. So, so good. How can this be? I have to have him in my mouth again.

But he's between my breasts, pumping hard. My saliva on his cock offers some lubrication but it dries fast and only his hot skin rubs against my breastbone. But before it starts to hurt, he groans and pulls away, vanishing from my perception. For a second, I'm disoriented again, lost without his body to give me direction.

Then his hand pushes me back onto the pillows and I flop, bouncing off the softness. He grips my hips; my panties vanish down my legs, pulled off faster than I could do it alone. And he's spreading my legs.

Is he going to fuck me? Will he pump into me the way he pumped between my breasts. "Please," I whimper. "Now. Please."

Fingers rub along the top of my stockings. A palm descends to my mound, grinding into my pussy. I whimper again, my back arching.

He's on top of me, covering me completely. His cock burns against my lower belly and I whimper, but his mouth covers mine. This kiss is deep, lingering, hungry. It rolls through my entire body, a wave of brilliance I've never experienced before. It's Tom. Only *Tom*.

Each of his touches is more possessive than the ones before. More demanding, as if he's losing patience. As if he truly, honestly wants me.

It makes me hotter.

"Fuck me, please. Tom! Now. I'm on the pill. Come in me. Please. I want you to come in me." I wrap my legs around him and push my feet into his hamstrings, making his hips grind against mine. I want him inside. I *need* him inside.

The noises he makes lack words but carry meaning: *Quiet.* The muscles of his shoulders tense under my hands. Tom breaks the force of my hold and his body pulls off mine.

"Tom!" Why is he doing this? "What's—"

His mouth descends onto my pussy and his tongue immediately finds my clit. I buck against him, my entire body suddenly, completely electric. I know he wants me to come. Now. Right now, as his fingers probe and his tongue dances. Before he's inside me.

The orgasm quakes me down to my bones. My throat constricts. My hands jitter. And Tom doesn't stop.

He licks and finger-fucks me, drawing my orgasm out into one shudder after another. How long it lasts, I don't know. I'm lost.

Until he takes a hold of a handful of breast again.

His cock is against my belly. He's flicking my nipple, and his mouth is working along my jaw, toward my earlobe. "You are beautiful. How can you be so beautiful?"

His words filter through me, washing over me like rain water. He's the beautiful one, my hard Tom. He dominates this moment. He dominates my world.

He's curled against me, rubbing, his muscles so tense I almost hear them hum.

I squirm, trying to move so when he pumps, he's pumping into me and not against my bellybutton. But he's holding me tight, his grip on my arms intense. He's not letting me move. And his thrusts become stronger, more powerful.

"Tom, in me. Please. Fuck me."

"*Ah!*" His head lifts away from my neck as his orgasm spurts onto my belly.

What just happened? Why didn't he come inside me? Confusion strangles my thoughts and I can't think. What did I do?

"Sammie," he whispers. He's still with me, holding on. His arms tighten.

I touch his head, feeling his soft hair. He's fiddling with the blindfold, untying it. When I see again, he's using the cloth to wipe his cum off my belly.

"Why?" I should be angry, but only confusion fills my head. He felt so good. Extraordinary. But I feel like something's missing, and it's not just him pumping into me.

I don't know what to say. I just don't want him to let go.

He makes a face like he doesn't want to talk.

This is complicated, I think. I've never dealt with complicated before. It's always been clear-cut fuck-and-go. Or fuck-and-sleep, like with Rick. But with Tom, it's more. He's kissing my forehead, his arms tight around my body.

I could run away. Go back to the loft. But Tom pulls me into his arms, even if he doesn't want to talk, and I don't want to be anywhere else.

I need to admit it. To myself. To him.

I curl around him. He feels warm, strong. Perfect. His skin, his body, his muscles, all fill my perception, my world, even without the blindfold.

I see, finally.

And I see Tom.

CHAPTER 12

Samantha

Full and glorious sun streams into the bedroom through the wide open curtains. I lay on his bed, naked, next to the beautiful and still sleeping Mr. Thomas Quidell. The bright morning dances over the strong, sculpted muscles of his back.

In the sunlight, I see what I couldn't last night. The sheet rides low on his hips, revealing a toned and perfect body. He's no longer the kid I fantasize about; he's someone I know in detail. But not full detail, the way I want it.

All I want to do is start in the center of his wonderful lower back, laying a kiss on his skin one inch at a time, up between his broad shoulders to the nape of his neck.

But I don't. He's snoring softly in that steady male way guys do when they lie on their stomachs. I should let him rest.

Carefully, I swing my feet over the side of the bed. A pile of clean and folded clothes sits on the top of his hand-me-down dresser, and I root through it, looking for a t-shirt. I don't want to put on my work clothes. It's Saturday morning and...

I look back at the bed. We didn't talk last night. We had sex—not penetration sex, but sex—and we didn't talk about it. He carried me into the bedroom instead, pulling me tight to him and kissing my forehead until we both fell asleep.

I didn't speak, either. We were together, in his bed, and for once I felt calm and safe. And I knew I could let my subconscious figure it all out.

I pull a t-shirt over my head. It's worn, old, with a fading logo of a nineties band on the front. It drops over my ass but I should find my panties. When he wakes up I'll ask to borrow some sweats.

He shifts a little and the bed groans. It's a comfortable mattress. I grin to myself, remembering those days right out of college when I, too, had no furniture.

I still don't. Everything in the loft belongs to Rick.

Frowning, I look down at my hands as my gut suddenly clenches up. I didn't end it with Rick before I left the bar with Tom. I didn't call. Hell, I didn't even send a text.

But I know why: revenge. And now I wonder if I'm just as shallow and flat as the man I'm about to leave behind.

Tom mumbles something, his deep baritone washing through the room as if carried on the sunlight, and I wonder how such a wonderful man—such a good person—could ever want to be with me.

Softly, I tiptoe out of the room. Sun streams into the living room as well, and his entire apartment is bright and shadow-free. It's cleaner than many bachelor's apartments, but that could be because he hasn't lived here long enough for the place to turn into a man cave.

But I don't see that happening. Tom is sensitive to his environment, and to what his environment brings to him.

Yet he still brought me home last night. Samantha Singleton, the fucked-up work fuck-buddy.

His sketchbook leans against the easel leg still. I pad over, the soles of my feet rubbing on the apartment's carpet, and pick it up.

There I am, half naked and stretched out on the pillows—and I'm beautiful. He's drawn me, arms out to him, my face full of contradictions. There's unvarnished, intense desire in my eyes. The tip of my head suggests uncertainty, but it's not in my body. He's what I need.

But he's hazed it, too, as if he can't quite see me. Like I'm hiding something from him.

I grip the sketchbook. He wouldn't have kept me in his bed all night if I was just some fuck buddy. And it's not what I want. I see it in this mirror he's made for me and I feel it all the way to my bones.

Standing here in the full glory of the light he throws on his life, I realize I need the light thrown on me, too. Because before, I couldn't see what I'd been groping for.

But will he tolerate me while I figure things out? I know, deep inside, hell, from *outside* too—from my skin and my elbows and my earlobes where he nibbled last night—I want him to. Sharing with him, being open no matter how scary it is, will be worth the pain.

The sounds of shuffling turn me around. Tom stands in the hallway, a pair of plaid sleep pants low on his gorgeous hips, and his hand rubbing across the top of his head. "Do you like it?" He points at the sketch.

I'd half expected him to ask why I'm still here, but I know that's not him. That's my own fears talking.

"Have you done gallery shows?" I hold out the book and the wondrous drawing. "You need to do gallery shows. This is beautiful. I've never seen anything like it."

He blinks, but a small grin works across his lips. "Do you want breakfast? I could make us eggs."

"I..." It's time to be open and honest, not just with him, but with everyone. And with myself. I look around for my phone. "I need to text Rick." It's not the most wholesome way to break—

Tom's face changes. Sadness rolls off his entire body. Anger creeps in, and his nostrils flare. He whispers, "*He* doesn't love you, Sammie."

I stop, frozen. Tom turns his back to me and takes a deep breath. Then he's gone, vanishing around the corner into the kitchen.

Did he...? I can't finish my own thought. I follow him into the kitchen.

He slaps a spatula onto the counter when I round the corner. "I didn't *fuck* you last night because I don't want it to be *fucking*. That's what it will be if you go back to him. Straight-up side-action fucking." He steps away from the counter, then back again. "Damn it, that's what it was, wasn't it? I wanted to be with you so badly I let last night happen even though I know you haven't made up your mind. I wanted to wake up next to you."

My mouth opens and closes. "You wanted to wake up next to me?"

He's watching me from his spot next to the counter, his jaw tight and his hand clenching the spatula. "Yes."

I realize this moment isn't just a test, it's *the* test. Am I going to be that woman he's afraid I am? The one who does side-action fucking? The one who lives with a guy because I like the sex and won't move out because...

And it's there, finally, in the front on my mind, a label on my little issues: because I think my main worth is the fucking.

I gasp, holding in a sob. Oh my God, how can that be? I'm doing well in my career. I'm happy with my friends and my life except when I'm not.

But I'm lonely. And I finally understand why.

"Sammie." Tom drops the spatula onto the counter and scoops me up into his big arms before I take another breath.

I can barely speak. How can I think such things? It's stupid. Tom doesn't see me that way. Though I am pretty sure Rick does.

And there's my answer to what's been feeding that stupid little thought.

"You're..." I curl against Tom's chest, my cheek pressed against his breastbone, over his heart. It beats strong and steady, like him. Strong, steady, and...

And accepting.

"What, Sammie?" His arms tighten around my waist, drawing me closer.

I don't finish my thought. I can't. I know what I'd say: *You're perfect. You're wonderful. You're better than I deserve.*

And *I think I'm falling in love with you.*

I'm terrified by this new thought. Will I ever deserve this man?

"I know what you're thinking." He speaks softly, into my hair. "You're thinking that you're fucked up again, aren't you?"

I nod against his chest, sniffling. My tears streak his skin but I don't want to let go. I don't want to move out of his embrace ever again.

"Then we take this one step at a time, okay?"

I nod again.

But I feel a small quake move through his body and his jaw tenses against my forehead. "What were you going to text to Rick?"

That I never want to see him again, I think. I so very much want to leave him—and the part of my life he represents—behind. "That I'm moving out. That I won't be there when he gets home tonight."

A quick, controlled sigh brushes against my hair. Tom's arms tighten again and for a moment, it's hard to breathe.

He's not letting me go. Even with all my fucked-upped-ness, he's holding on.

I kiss his jaw, holding on for dear life. He threw me a life preserver and I'm not going to lose it. I'm not going to ruin this. "Can I store my stuff here until I find a place to live? I don't have a lot."

A snort pops against the skin over my ear. "You can stay here as long as you want. Not just your stuff. You." He backs away enough to look me in the eye. "If you need space, I'll sleep on the couch."

I giggle as much from the release of tension as from his chivalrousness. "You don't have a couch."

"Then I will blow up the air mattress and sleep on the floor. I'm not letting you go. And I'm not letting you run away, either. I'm a Quidell. We fight for what we want." He pulls me back into his arms.

I bury my face in his chest, even though my head's spinning.

"Sammie." A gentle kiss touches my temple. Another falls on my cheek. When I lift my chin, yet another brushes my lips. "We'll take this slow, okay? So we're both sure."

I nod, not speaking. He's right. Figuring this out will take some time.

Another warm, sweet kiss finds my mouth. "Let's get your things."

Tom takes my hand to help me into my future.

CHAPTER 13

Thomas

"How did you live in this dungeon?" I ask Sammie. How someplace as architecturally interesting as her building could be rendered so deeply dark and soulless, I do not understand. Yet here I stand in the huge, open center space wondering if I'm about to hear bats flitting around the ceiling.

Sammie kisses my cheek as she sets another box next to the door. She's filled storage containers, laundry baskets, even plastic grocery bags and I've been hauling them down to the truck. All that's left is an antique table lamp from her grandmother and a wide assortment of frozen dinners.

"No you don't." I scowl at the bag holding the contents of the freezer. "You don't need this crap. I'm going to feed you well." Looking her up and down, I give her my best charming grin. "How can you be so blazing hot when you eat this stuff?"

She laughs, grinning back at me. "And how am I supposed to 'take it slow' when you're always flirting with me?"

How am I supposed to *not* flirt with her? Running up and down in the elevator has kept my mind occupied, but my balls ache. The "taking it slow" is excruciating.

She laughs again when I don't answer. My face must have given me away. But a hint of nervousness filters through with her chuckle. She must still feel uneasy about all this.

I jam my hands into my pockets. "I'm sorry. I don't mean to—"

A kiss silences my apology. It's quick—she's out of reach before I can wrap my arms around her—but it's still a kiss. I grin again, watching her put the frozen dinners back in the freezer.

"I'll leave the bad food, how's that sound?" She slams the door and looks around the kitchen one last time.

Leave the bad food here. And all the bad memories, I think. She needs to leave it all behind, especially Rick the dick.

The cat—Mickles, she calls him—rubs against my shin. He's a sweet fluffy animal and every time I come in, he meows a greeting.

"Is Mr. Pickles coming too?" I pick him up, stroking his back. "He likes me. See?" The cat headbutts my chin and I scratch his ears, doing my best to make her some new, good memories.

Sammie watches for a long second. Her face softens and she smiles a sweet, wonderful smile. "He was wandering outside shortly after I moved in. Rick brought him in, so I've always thought of him as Rick's cat. But I'm the one who takes care of him."

"She calls you Mickles, did you know that?" I rub under the kitty's chin. "You let her get away with that? Have you no dignity, man?"

Mickles meows his answer and headbutts me again.

Sammie laughs. "And here I thought he was aloof and standoffish. He's never like that with Rick."

"Well then, I shall liberate the woman *and* the cat." Bowing, I look around. "Got a carrier for him?"

I get a thrill from stealing the douchebag's cat. Juvenile, I know. But I'm not leaving the kitty here to have him end up on the street again.

"It's in the hall closet." She points down the dark corridor.

This place really is a cave.

Sammie opens the cabinet door next to her head. "I'll get his food and dishes. There's a bag of litter in the closet. Grab it too, please."

Nodding, I set down Mickles and walk away, toward the kitty's carrier. We'll be out of here in a minute or so, and then she's mine. She can take as long as she wants to ease into it, but it's going to happen. Her key to this place and a note are already on the kitchen table.

I have a couple of sleepless nights ahead of me, knowing she's nearly naked in my bed, by herself. Maybe touching herself as she thinks about me. God knows I'm going to be touching myself. I shift as I walk, hoping she doesn't take *too* long.

I hear the front door open. Sammie must be taking another load down to the—

"Rick!"

I stop, my hand inches from the closet doorknob. The son of a bitch is back. Early.

Every inch of my body screams to march in there right now and punch the douchebag. But acting like some uncivilized freak will just chase Sammie away. So I don't. My arm tightens, wanting that punch, but I won't.

"What are you doing?" I hear a male voice. He sounds more annoyed than angry.

"You texted me, not your booty call last week, Rick." Sammie sounds strong, not frightened.

"So?"

I turn around. I can't be in the hallway, with her alone with him.

"What did you think I was going to do?" But her voice is strong and she's holding it together. I feel a rush of pride, though I know I don't have a right to.

Rick drops something onto the floor and a boom reverberates through the loft. "I don't know. Ask to join us?"

I stomp down the hall. Even if I don't punch him, he needs to know I'm here.

"Who'd you bring in here?"

"None of your business, Rick." Fear is creeping into her voice.

"It's my business who you bring into *my* place, you little bitch."

"Little bitch?" Sammie sounds shocked. "Have I always been a *little bitch* to you?"

"You're surprised? And here I thought you liked it."

When I round the corner, he's standing over her, his posture dominant and threatening. He's muscular like an athlete, but I'm bigger.

"Leave her alone," I growl.

Rick looks up, his eyes narrow. "I'm not the only one with some side action, huh?" He steps away from Sammie.

She's shaking. I walk to her, my gaze not leaving Rick, and pull her against my side.

The need to punch him—punch *anything*—makes my shoulders tense.

Sammie steps in front of me, her back against my chest, like she's protecting *me*.

When she speaks, her voice is low. "He's a million times a better man than you, Rick."

She's against me and I feel her shaking grow. She can't be here anymore. I curl my arms around her waist. She doesn't need him cutting her down.

"Let's go," I whisper.

Her arms fold over mine. "He's a million times a better person than me."

Rick snorts. "*Everyone* is a better person than you, sweetheart."

He's glaring at her, not looking at me, and I think that if she'd come here alone, he would have hit her. Her breath hitches.

"Don't listen to him." I want to tell her the truth—that she has a beautiful heart and wonderful mind and that I'm falling in love with her. That she's worth so much more than how this asshole makes her feel. "You're my muse," I whisper.

Sammie turns in my arms, her eyes huge, but she doesn't speak. A tear appears on her lashes and all I want to do is to kiss it away. All I want right now is to pick her up and take her out of here.

I look over her shoulder, right at the son of a bitch. I'm trying not to yell, but it comes out loud anyway. "You're a fucking idiot."

I pull Sammie closer.

Rick laughs. "Sure thing, bro."

If she hadn't been between us, I would have hit him. But she holds onto me and she's more important. Much more important.

She doesn't turn around. "Do not contact me again, Rick."

He pulls his wallet out of his pocket and tosses it onto the table. "Get out, you little skank. If I find anything of yours left behind, I'm burning it."

He flips us off and walks away, into the living room.

And I all but carry Sammie out of there.

CHAPTER 14

Samantha

T om slams the back of his truck. On my lap, Mickles circles inside his carrier and lets out a frightened little whimper.

I don't blame the kitty. I want to whimper, too.

Tom's taking me to his place. He refused to let me go back up to the loft after putting Mickles in the carrier. He went in by himself to get my grandmother's lamp. I sat in the truck for an agonizing fifteen minutes, terrified that he and Rick would get into a fight and Tom would end up in jail because of me. But he appeared again, the lamp in one hand and the bag of cat litter in the other, and finished packing the truck.

He opens the driver's side door and stands there, looking at me with more concern on his face than I've ever seen from a boyfriend. "Are you going to be alright?"

My own thought buzzes in my head. *Boyfriend*. I obviously mean more to him than just a fuck buddy. A lot more. A million times more.

"Honey, are you okay?" He crawls in but doesn't start the truck.

I nod *yes*. "Thank you."

Tom leans across the shift and gently kisses my cheek. "You *are* my muse. Please believe that."

My mouth opens and I suck in my breath. What's going to happen when he realizes I'm not as good a person as he is? Will he kick me out, too?

The truck starts and he pulls out onto the street. We head back to his place, silent except for Mickles's meowing.

"Everything he said is bullshit, Sammie." He's watching traffic and not me. "I am not a million times better than you. Him? Fuck, yeah. But you? No." Tom throws me one of his disarming grins.

This handsome man wants me to be his muse. He wants me to live with him and be his friend and his lover. But mostly he wants me to be happy.

My breath hitches but I hold in the tears. I'm a fucking mess.

"Tell you what. I'll stop and we'll get a pint of that extra thick, extra chocolaty ice cream and call it dinner, okay?" Another disarming grin comes my way.

I laugh. I can't help myself. "You said no bad food." He's trying so hard to make everything better. It's working, too.

"Since when is chocolate bad food? It's therapy." He winks. "At least that's what I see all my female relatives say on social media."

I laugh again. How can he make me feel so much better so fast? It's like he's magic.

Which, I'm beginning to suspect, he is. If I found some sort of supernatural being when I first saw him as a freshman. "Did you put a spell on me all those years ago when you drew that first picture?"

Now Tom laughs. "Why yes, m'lady, I did. And the only way to break it is to eat ice cream with me." He glances over again as he pulls into the grocery store parking lot. "You, my beautiful Sammie, are about to be treated to a good meal. One I cook special for you."

"Oh?" He has that happy look to him again, like when he gave me the first drawing. He's put what happened with Rick behind him, even if I haven't yet.

"Your new life awaits and I intend to celebrate." He rolls down the windows. "So that neither you nor Mickles become uncomfortable while I'm inside purchasing secret ingredients for our special meal."

Opening the door, he hops out. "I shall return to you momentarily, my sweet."

As I watch him walk into the store, I breathe deep for the first time since we left the loft, and I realize Tom rescued me. Not during the altercation with Rick—that, he let me handle myself. I needed to handle it myself. I needed to see just how much Rick didn't care.

But Tom does. And just now, here, in his truck, he offered me another a life preserver so I don't drown in the residue of the hell I just left behind. The hell of my own making that I've been wallowing in.

I scratch Mickles's fur through the door of his carrier. "What do you think, my fluffy friend?"

The cat answers with a questioning meow.

"Yeah, I think you're right. I think I better not screw this up." I sit up straight in the seat. I'm leaving the fucked-up me behind, in the loft, with Rick. Tom's right—I need to own not just my libido but all my wants and desires. And right now, I want my lover to also be my friend.

I want intimacy with my sex. I want to wake up with the sun.

I want Tom.

❦

TOM WENT ALL OUT. THE WHOLE MEAL SMELLED AS GOOD AS IT looked. The steak was the best I've tasted in a long time, as were the potatoes and the salad and the wine. He even managed to coax Mickles out from under the bed for his dinner.

We ate on the floor again, next to his easel, with one of my boxes between us acting as a table.

I sit back, watching him. I feel relaxed, floating in a warm wine buzz. I hold up the tumbler for a bit more. "We need to get you some proper stemware."

"Hmm..." He takes another sip.

I tap the box. "And you need a table."

"Sounds like we need to go shopping." The *we* rolls off his tongue, accented lightly by his baritone, and he smiles.

He's beyond handsome. My body has been responding to his gaze and his touch all evening and it's been driving me insane. Everything tightens. My mouth waters and I feel new moisture between my thighs.

It's different this time. My desire for him feels deeper, as if it's coming from everywhere and not just from my erogenous zones.

But if I'm honest with myself, I'll admit that it *isn't* different. I'm just admitting it for the first time. He's caused this reaction from me since the first moment I met him and up until now, I didn't want to think about it.

Because I didn't think it was real. No man who saw only my tits would laugh and smile with me, or comfort me the way he has, or would have rescued my cat, too. Or want to take me shopping for housewares.

He helped me unpack, made dinner, even served the ice cream first. We talked about work and our favorite movies and how we're going to get him into a gallery.

He'd stood still for a long moment, watching me, the most wonderful grin on his face.

The same way he's looking at me right now.

I'm his muse.

"I'd like to go shopping with you," I whisper.

His smile widens. For the first time, I see what Tom looks like when he's truly happy.

My heart feels as if it's going to burst out of my chest.

"Tomorrow?" He stands and picks up our dirty dishes.

I follow him into the little kitchen, watching his flawlessly proportioned backside. I'd rather spend my Sunday rubbing my hands over his ass again while nibbling on his little line of body hair descending from his navel to his oh-so-perfect cock, but shopping could be fun, too.

We chat about what he needs for his apartment as he washes and I dry the dishes. Twice, he leans over and kisses my cheek. By the time the last dish returns to the cupboard, we have all of Sunday planned.

It feels good. He wants to be with me, not just fuck me, and for once in my life I feel wanted.

He pulls me tight to his chest. "I'm happy you're here, Sammie. I'm happy you decided to stay with me and not with someone else."

Under my hands, his lower back feels strong and powerful. Against my cheek, his heart beats strong and comforting. Stubble rubs against my hair but it's nice. He smells of cooking and washing dishes and the afternoon's work, but it's good. It's life with him.

Once again, I feel luckier than I deserve. I kiss his jaw, hoping he understands how much I want to be with him. All of him is hard against me—his abdomen, his arms, the bulge in his pants. He strokes my back sensuously as he buries his face in my hair.

But he pulls away. "Mickles and I will sleep in the living room tonight." Tom waves his hand before grasping mine. "So you can settle in."

I blink. The hunger in his eyes mirrors the hunger I feel, but he's not taking advantage. He's not pulling me into the bedroom.

And I don't know what to say.

CHAPTER 15

Thomas

Sammie doesn't say much as she unpacks her stuff in the bathroom. I hear clinks and clatters as items fill up the countertop and appear in my shower. Her toothbrush whirs and the water runs before she steps out again, wearing an old pair of sweats and a worn t-shirt.

With her hair down, her face fresh, she's more beautiful than I've ever seen her before. Her skin glows. The t-shirt hugs her breasts and I want to pick her up and back her against the wall. I want to rip off the shirt with my teeth.

But she needs to feel that I want her here for more reasons than the promise of great sex. No matter how I feel, no matter what I say, I know I need to demonstrate my intentions. And I need her to demonstrate hers.

It'll kill me to get into a relationship with her only to find out six months down the road she never really wanted one in the first place. I can't lose my heart. Not like Dan did.

I fluff my pillow and the small and uncomfortable air mattress squeaks. "Good night, Sammie."

She watches me with her big eyes for a long moment, then nods. Before I know it, she's down the hall. The lights go out in the bedroom.

I turn off the lights in the living room. The room is still bright—I haven't closed the curtains. Nor will I. The moon is full tonight and fills the sky with a silver sheen. If I'm to lay here on my brother's squeaky air mattress, at least the heavens can keep me company.

Mickles appears next to my head, purring. I scratch his ears until he seems satisfied and walks away, down the hall. Looks like the kitty sleeps with Sammie, even if I don't.

My mind wanders to memories of her moaning under me, her cheeks and lips flushed, her nipples tight nubs. Damn, she felt exquisite. So soft against my cock.

My hand finds my lengthening shaft. I could go in there. I could go into the bedroom and pull back the blankets. Strip off her sweats right now. Suck her clit into my mouth. Flick it with my tongue. Make her scream my name.

I want *her* rubbing me right now. I want to make her understand how much I want her.

From the other room, I hear the bed groan. My hand freezes.

Mickles meows.

I sit up and pull the blanket over my erection when I hear her walk down the hall. The last thing I want is for her to feel obliged. I know she likes sex—I like sex, especially with her—but it can't be just sex. Not with her.

Sammie stops in a pool of moonlight, shimmering as if she'd descended from heaven. She's more beautiful than any angel with her hair flowing over her shoulders and her skin glowing in the silver light. I blink, staring at her, unable to speak.

"Tom?" She shuffles slightly and I hear her bare feet on the carpet.

She took off the sweats. She's standing in my hallway wearing only the t-shirt and her panties, my muse. My goddess.

I groan. I don't mean to, but it escapes.

Her foot slides over the carpet again. "Thank you for being a gentleman." Her hand grips the corner where the hallway meets the living room wall. "You've given me something no man has ever given me before—I feel valued."

Her hand smooths across her belly and the t-shirt hitches up along her hip. I see her tiny panties and her lovely skin. But mostly I see her body language. I see the trust she's giving me.

"Part of my head is screaming I don't deserve you. But I don't want to fall victim to that any longer. Because that's what's been happening. A part of me used to think Rick was right."

"No, Sammie—"

She holds up her hand, silencing me. "But you're telling me something completely different. It feels good, Tom. It feels healthy and so much better. I feel right with you. Happy. And..." A small sniffle pops between her words. "And I want to see you happy. I *want* to be your muse."

She steps forward and her feet move out of the pool of silver. The light travels up her long legs, over her torso, and across her breasts. And when she stops, I see her face clearly.

She's looking at me with more affection than I've ever seen from a woman. More caring. More desire to make this work than I could ever hope for. And more genuine desire for me.

Her hand extends and she reaches. For me. "Please come to bed."

I'm off the damned air mattress and in her arms before either of us can take a breath. I scoop her up.

"Sammie," I whisper. Her breath tickles my neck as she wraps her legs and arms around me. I grip her backside, holding her up as I back her against the wall.

I kiss her with everything I feel, on her lips, her cheeks, her neck.

She moans, gasping, and pulls me in for a deeper kiss. Our lips dance, our tongues touching, mingling. She tastes of mint and femininity; smells of sweet soap and sex.

My beautiful Sammie tangles her fingers in my hair and I feel the fire of her skin, the hard buttons of her nipples, the heat of her body pressing against my cock.

And I want her so much I grind against her belly as I hold her to the wall. It's too much. I'm going insane.

"Take off the t-shirt." She moans again as she paws at the fabric covering my torso.

I lean back enough for her to pull it up. Wiggling one arm out, I switch the hand gripping her ass and she pulls the shirt over my head and down my shoulder.

A low growl rolls from her throat when she runs her fingers over my biceps. "Damn, you are *gorgeous*."

I chuckle and nip her earlobe. "I'm going to fuck you unconscious."

The low, stuttered breath of a response almost sends me over the edge. Right here, with me holding her on the wall and rubbing against her through my flannel pajamas and her damned panties.

I drop her legs to the floor.

She holds tight to my neck, refusing to let go. "Tom! Now. Please." Her mouth works across my chest and she scrapes her teeth first across one nipple, then the other.

I don't usually like such play but when she does it, it feels like she's setting off a volcano under my skin.

"Damn, woman." I pull her t-shirt over her head, stopping for a moment when the fabric curls around her wrists. Her breasts thrust out at me, wonderfully etched by the moon's shadows, and I drop my mouth to her left nipple.

"Don't stop." She's breathing heavy now, almost panting.

I tongue her nipple, suckling and biting. She shudders under my touch and I barely hold it together. I need to be in her. Now. But first I'm going to prove to her that she made the right choice.

Her t-shirt drops to the floor as I drop to my knees in front of her. I hook the lace of her panties and yank, pulling them down her thighs.

The last time when I went down on her she tasted sweet, and I want more. I grind the heel of my palm into her clit and she moans again. Her fingers tangle deeper into my hair and flex against my scalp.

I lick.

"Oh my God the real you is a thousand times better than any fantasy." Her fingers flex again.

Surprised, I stop tonguing her beautiful, sweet pussy. "What?"

Sammie blinks, her face saying what she doesn't vocalize: *Oh, shit.*

"You fantasize about me?" My inner teenager is dancing around yelling *That's right, baby!* and *Oh hell yeah!* Sammie thinks about me when she gets off. Not that douchebag and not some movie star. *Me.*

"For four years."

I blink up at her, stunned. Four years? That means... "Since you saw me on campus? When I drew the first picture of you?"

She nods.

The stupidest thought possible parades through my head: *I win.* I won before I even met her. I won the lotto four years ago and I'm just now finding out.

I must be smiling like an idiot because she is smiling at me, her beautiful face warm and happy. She tugs on my shoulders and this time I don't argue. I stand, taking her in a new, deep kiss.

"I think..." I'm kissing her so hard, she can barely speak. "...I've always..." I pinch her nipple. She shudders and I pull her breath from her with another kiss. "...known it would be you."

She feels right against me, holding me, wanting me. And I think, finally, all the ugliness that asshole made her feel has vanished. She's here with me. Completely, totally with *me.*

"I'm falling in love with you, Tom."

CHAPTER 16

Samantha

He didn't let go when I said it. He didn't drop me or pull away or run. He picked me up again.

My wonderful Tom, his eyes as silver and beautiful as the moonlight spilling in through the balcony door, holds the naked me against his rock hard body, his face buried against my neck and his stubble rubbing the delicate skin of my shoulder.

"Promise me you'll stay." I barely hear his whisper. "Promise me you're not going to decide in a year and a half that you're bored."

What am I supposed to say? I would never—

The realization of what he means drops on me like a cascade of rocks. This is about his brother's divorce.

He might be holding me in the air, his arms curled around my body and his hands gripping my bottom, but he's the vulnerable one, not me. If I'm careless, I'll rip his heart to shreds.

I will never be careless with this man.

"You are not boring." I kiss along his hairline. "You are the opposite of boring."

He chuckles against my neck and his deep baritone vibrates over my skin. I moan, feeling an orgasm build out here in the hallway, in this pool of moonlight.

I've found what I've been missing all these years. What I've been looking for but never thought I deserved. "I'm the luckiest woman alive." I found Tom.

"Sammie," he whispers.

I kiss him with everything he's given me. "You are better than any fantasy and I really do love you." With everything I have.

I drown in his next kiss. How can I be so lucky? He's with me, around me, and I so very much need him inside me.

"Please, Tom. Now. Don't tease me anymore."

"Tease you?" He's growl-chuckling in my ear. "You wear a matching indigo bra and skirt and you accuse *me* of teasing?"

He paid enough attention to *notice*? "I want you *right now*, Thomas! Now! Damn it—"

I drop toward the floor, fast. He's flipped me and I'm about to skid on the carpet, but he slows my descent. I land with the most beautiful man on the planet looking down at me, his face intense and fierce and showing just how much he wants to be with me.

"Tom!" I'd rather die than hurt him. He's everything. My soul.

"Sammie." He frees himself from his flannel sleep pants and the next thing I know the head of his hard shaft is pressing against my opening.

My nails dig into his buttocks. He moves into me slowly, sliding carefully, making sure he's not hurting me. His lips glide over to my ear. He kisses, his breath hot and full of desire.

"Sammie, I love you." He pumps, filling me completely, and I slide along the carpet, my back heating.

I'm with him. Where I should be, in a splash of moonlight under an open window. With my Tom. "I love you, too," I say, loud and clear. "I love you."

He pulls almost completely out. I feel the head of his cock rub around my opening and then he's inside me again, burying himself all the way to his hilt.

I almost scream, he feels so good. I've never had a man so deep before, never so intense. He fits inside me perfectly, stretching me almost to the point it hurts, but not quite. Tom holds me just before the pleasure becomes pain.

My back arches when he pumps into me again and I moan, shuddering. His mouth descends to mine and all my breath leaves me, lifted away by the god who takes me hard, right now, on the carpet in the hallway of his tiny apartment.

"Tom," I whisper. His name is all I can say.

His gaze never leaves my face. He thrusts and I moan and I don't want this to end.

No man other than Tom will ever touch me again. No man could possibly match what he does to me.

My orgasm knocks me back and I lose all sense of the world. I feel only Tom's body pressing into mine, hear only his ragged groans. It floods me but I know he's building toward his own climax. He doesn't stop and I don't want him to. I want him to come inside me. I want to see his face in ecstasy.

He kisses me again, breathing into my mouth. His breath is hot, full of desire. Full of passion. And I kiss him back.

Groaning, his back arches. His orgasm rocks through his body and I feel myself responding, another taking me. They reverberate between us, and we both gasp, holding tight to each other.

Tom is beautiful, his handsome face full of happiness and life. Tom, my lover. Tom, my love.

He drops on top of me, his strength spent. But I don't push him off. I pull him closer.

We lay on the floor, curled around each other. His body regains its center and he smiles, his blue-green eyes warm and happy. His fingers trace my cheek.

I'm happy for the first time in years.

"So much for taking it slow." He kisses the bridge of my nose.

I grin, my fingers tracing his cheek. "I think I like being a cougar."

Tom laughs and his cock bobs inside me. It's one of the most wonderful sensations I've ever felt.

His face takes on an expression of mock seriousness. "You liked that, didn't you?" Seriousness and hunger.

I can't stop a moan from escaping. My younger lover isn't going to let me rest. Smiling, I run my hands up and down his spine. His eyes flutter and his shoulders release. Tom drops again, his full weight pressing down on me.

"*You* liked *that*, didn't you?" I'm just as mock serious.

Grinning, he kisses me again. "I don't want to sleep on the air mattress tonight."

He's never sleeping anywhere except next to me. Not tonight. Not tomorrow night. Not any night.

When we stand in the moonlight, I curl into his embrace. I run my palm over his arms, his solid shoulders, and up onto his head. I wrap my fingers in his hair.

Tom kisses me with more passion, more real desire than any man ever before has and I know this is right. This is perfect.

The moon glides across the sky. When we finally sleep, he lies next to me, sated, his arm over my belly.

I kiss his forehead, just as sated.

And finally, after all this time, happy.

CHAPTER 17

Thomas

A ndy hands me a glass of champagne. Like Sammie, he's far too smart to be working in Campaign Relations but he waves his hand in the air and says some cliché about "house payments" any time someone brings it up.

Except when Sammie asked for his help after she took on repping my work. He spent a full hour looking at my paintings and drawings and by the end of the day he'd called five of his contacts.

That was seven months ago. Now, when he's not fetching booze, he mingles with the guests at my first gallery show.

"So, you two set a date yet?" He points with his champagne flute at the life-sized painting of my fiancé. In it, Sammie leans back, one leg dipped into a lake and the other propped up, her luscious body covered only in a black bikini bottom. One arm covers her breasts. But the true beauty of the painting isn't her form, it's the happiness I captured in her face. The golds, oranges, and reds of the sunset cascade over her skin, but she's looking at me. And she's smiling.

"We're thinking spring." I'd marry her right now but her family in Grand Forks will never forgive her if they can't plan the whole affair.

To my surprise, they don't seem all that put off by the number of nudes she has sat for, though her father, who's already consumed three full glasses of champagne, has spent the entire evening blushing.

Andy nods. "If you two elope, I will never forgive you." He frowns and nods toward an older couple I don't recognize. "Your adoring fans want an *event*."

I chuckle. Without Sammie's communications work and Andy's contacts, none of this would have been possible.

Andy pats my arm. "Off I go to sell, sell, sell!" Winking, he walks away.

I hear a little boy's hushed voice and I turn around, instinctively kneeling.

"Uncle Tommy!" Bart, dressed in a tuxedo t-shirt and black pants, one of his action figures gripped by its leg, runs into my arms.

I hoist him up. "Aren't you up past your bedtime?"

He stares at the painting. He's been talking nonstop about the show for two months. Dan and I had a long talk about a five-year-old and naked lady paintings, especially when that naked lady was going to be his new aunt, but we both agreed he'd never forgive us if we left him out. So I made sure Andy set out a couple of my portraits of him, and also some of his drawings of his toys, in the special "Bart" corner.

Dan sat him down and told him exactly how he was to act and that he was to stay out of the main gallery unless either Dan or I was with him. And the difference between paintings and photos. Plus a few other things. He's been an exceptional little man all evening, listening and following directions, and charmed many guests with his ever-widening understanding of art.

Bart leans close to my ear. "Sammie is pretty."

I laugh. Yep, my nephew is most definitely a Quidell man.

He looks over my shoulder. "Ms. Frasier is prettier." He's developed quite the crush on his art teacher.

"Well, at least I know you won't be stealing Sammie from me."

"Uncle Tommy!" Bart pushes his fists into his hips when I set him down. "Stealing is bad."

Dan rounds a display, the pretty Ms. Frasier next to him. Bart, making a show of behaving, walks stiffly to his father.

Dan hoists him up. "I think someone is tired."

Bart yawns. "I'm not tired."

Camille—Ms. Frasier—nods to me as she takes Bart from Dan. "Well done, Tom." Bart snuggles in, obviously happy his favorite teacher came along to keep him company.

I nod back. "Thank you."

"Dinner tomorrow?" Dan sticks his hands in his pockets. My poor brother looks uncomfortable in his suit, though I've noticed he's upped his grooming game these past few weeks.

I glance at Camille again. She's talking with Bart, giving him her full attention. Dan runs his fingers through his hair, watching them too, and he looks happy.

"Dinner it is, then. But no mac and cheese this time, okay?"

Bart giggles. "I *like* mac and cheese."

Sammie appears, gliding around the same display. Her indigo dress hugs her curves and she's as luminescent in real life as she is in the painting. Smiling, she pats Camille's arm and ruffs Bart's hair. "Someone looks tired."

Bart yawns again. "I'm not *tired*."

Sammie laughs and kisses my nephew's cheek. "You have been a very good Quidell tonight. We are all proud of you, young man."

Bart beams.

"We will see you tomorrow for dinner, okay?" Sammie musses his hair again.

My little nephew nods. "Okay, Auntie Sammie."

She blinks, backing toward me. This is the first time Bart has called her "Auntie." I take her hand, squeezing. My beautiful Sammie beams as much as Bart, and, I do believe, she is just as happy.

We watch them go. Sammie leans against my shoulder, her cheek pressed against my arm. Her soft floral perfume wraps around me, adding an extra touch of femininity to her already perfect female form.

She squeezes my hand. "The first time he asks Camille to sit for him, your brother's going to freak out."

"Probably." I kiss the top of her head. "But I bet he'll draw a spectacular picture."

She looks up, smiling. "Andy says we can leave, if you want to."

"Oh?" Her dress is loose at the neckline and I have an exceptional view of her cleavage. Leaving sounds like just what I need right now.

"But first I want you to come down the street with me." Sammie tugs on my hand, leading me out the door.

It's too cold to be out without our coats and the sidewalk is slick, but she laughs and pulls me into the night air. The city feels alive tonight. People bustle by, most looking at Sammie and her bare arms, some laughing. Our breath freezes and Sammie snuggles close. I loop my arm over her shoulder.

The shops all brim with shoppers and the skyline twinkles. Music blasts from the restaurant down the street, along with the smell of burgers and fries. The cold air makes the blues bluer and the reds crisper, and I think, when we get home, I'll paint my Sammie in her dress under the winter night sky.

A block down, she produces a key from her clutch and pulls me into a dark stairwell. Shadows fall over us, but she shines, and lifting her against the wall would add a wonderful cap to the evening.

But she's laughing and up the stairs, out of sight, before I can yank up her skirt.

"Sammie?" I hear her heels clinking on a wood floor.

The lights are off but I see the space clearly. It's huge, with one full wall of floor-to-ceiling windows. The city lights pour in, flooding the entire wide area with golds and silvers and the reflected red and green of a neon sign across the street.

To one side, an open bookcase blocks the view of an old desk that has been pushed against the wall, and between the shelves I see Sammie's blue dress.

I stare at her for a moment, through the shelves, realizing that even though we aren't in a library, this moment is very much like her school fantasy. The one she's described for me now. Several brilliant times.

I'm immediately hard. I step out from behind the case. Sammie leans back on the desk and my palms find her breasts. I rub, watching her bite her lip. "Let me see." It's cold in here but her skin feels volcanic. I hitch up her skirt. "I want to see."

She's not wearing panties. All night, my exquisite Sammie has been walking around my gallery opening in her bright blue, clinging dress without panties.

I stare at the v between her legs, my mind totally lost.

Sammie smiles and undoes my belt. Is she going to suck me off? I want to be in her. I want to kiss her while I fuck her. My beautiful Sammie.

"You want to see?" she whispers into my mouth.

"I want *you*."

She gasps when I pound into her. Damn, she feels tight. I hold her legs and she screams my name and when we both come, I collapse on top of her. She's given us both that perfect end to a perfect evening.

Sammie wraps her legs around my hamstrings and holds me inside her. "What do you think of this space?"

"Hmm?" She smells good and I'm not thinking anymore. She's intoxicated me.

"It's nice, isn't it?" She kisses my cheek and wiggles.

I pull out even though I don't want to.

"I thought you'd like the windows."

I glance around once I've readjusted my clothes. It is a beautiful space. During the day, the light coming in would be perfect for painting.

"With both our salaries, we can afford it." She's watching my face as she readjusts her dress. "It's zoned residential. We could renovate. Live here."

My beautiful Sammie found this place with its open view and its wide spaces. She found it for *us*. "It's available?"

"I thought maybe we could paint that wall orange." She points to a little jut-out next to the windows. "If you don't think it will bother you while you're painting." Sammie skips into the red and green light thrown by the sign across the street. "This whole area here should be your studio!"

Her dress swirls around her legs as she turns in a circle, her arms out, like a ballerina. She dances in the red and the green, my muse in blue.

All I want—all I will ever want, from this moment forward—is to see her the way she is now. Happy and alive and spinning in the moonlight, for me. The light I will never block from her life. "I love you, Ms. Samantha Singleton, Sammie for short."

I scoop up the woman I love. The woman who makes everything worthwhile.

Sammie laughs and kisses me with all the passion in her soul. All the warmth and the joy she's always had. And can now express.

"I love you too, Mr. Thomas, Tom Quidell." She snuggles against my chest. "I love you very much."

The Story continues
in book two, **Daniel's Fire**

Ex-firefighter Dan Quidell fights to hold his life together after a divorce and career-ending injury. Then he meets Camille Frasier....

DANIEL'S FIRE PREVIEW

CHAPTER ONE

Daniel

My truck's service indicator winks on as I pull into the lot of my son's daycare. Frowning, I park outside the big Community Center building and stare at the little blue wrench and the letter-number combo on my dash. It's one of the expensive service reminders. One involving every filter and hose attached to my truck's engine, and from my last check, it probably means new tires as well.

I pull the key and sit back, mentally adding "take in the truck" to the cloud of nag inside my head. Most people would call it a mental to-do list. To me, it's a massing zombie scene: I'm on the rooftop and each time I tick something off the list, I get an undead kill shot.

Most days, I get more of them than they get bites out of me.

It's a violent way to keep a to-do list, I know. But visualization is one of the techniques they taught me while I laid on my back in that damned hospital recovering after the doctors inserted pins into my shoulder. And my thigh. And layered on the skin grafts. My doc told me if popping the heads off slow, lumbering zombies helps decrease my stress level, then by all means I should pop away.

Both my brothers think it's hilarious. Some guys have stacks of porn on the top shelves of their bedroom closets. I have stacks of shitty movies because my little brother Rob buys every idiotic zombie DVD he finds.

I glance up at the wide steel and concrete expanse of the Community Center's boxlike, early nineties architecture. My kid's in there right now, laughing and playing with the other four-year-olds, and I can't help but think that I need to up my game. Life's got too many shitty zombies. I have a boy to protect.

I look at the sun, feeling its warmth for a second, and breathe in. The air smells fresh, though the highway is on the other side of the hill and the road noise hums through the lot. A summer breeze blows and the occasional cloud keeps it from getting too hot. It's a nice day.

I count, because it's another technique the doc at the hospital taught me. To understand the moment. To see what's really here. And to live.

Sometimes it's hard. But I do it. I have a kid.

Bart's daycare teacher—the amazing Ms. Cunningham, who used to teach high school English before "retiring" to organize and run the community-based daycare—set up a strawberry picking field trip for all the kids at the center. She called me personally, claiming I was one of her favorite students back in the day, and asked if I would like to come along.

Who am I to say no to Ms. Cunningham? Besides, I get to spend time with my kid *and* watch the pretty young teachers sticking out their sweet round asses while they bend over to pick berries.

I may not have stacks of porn in my closet, but I'm still a man. Even if my scars and my life have shut down dating.

I slam the truck door and lean against the front fender, stretching my hamstring. I changed into cargo shorts and a long-sleeved t-shirt before driving over. At the time, I didn't notice that the scar on my leg was visible.

My brothers tell me not to be so self-conscious. But, like seeing what's really here, sometimes it's hard.

I walk toward the Community Center door. The aches are bad

today, even with the nice weather. Maybe the flavor of fresh berries on the tongue and the laughter of little kids will ease at least some of it.

I can hope.

❧

Camille

FORTY PRE-KINDERGARTENERS, SIX TEACHERS AND AIDES, AND EIGHT parents. That's three kids per adult. I hand over a bright green t-shirt and the corresponding green kids' shirts to Ms. Selby, the pregnant parent standing in front of my table, in the middle of the Community Center lobby. She's pretty. Wearing designer yoga maternity wear, too. Her perfume smells like an expensive field of handcrafted French lavender. Or how I imagine a field of expensive Old World lavender tended only by the most artisanal hands would smell. The closest I'll ever get to France is downloaded movies and the occasional glass of fine wine.

"I'm supposed to put this on?" Smiling, though she's obviously annoyed by the chaotic green of the shirt, she holds it like she would a pair of stinky workout shoes.

"It's so your group can easily identify you. And you, them." I point to the three little kid shirts and her assigned list before pointing toward the room she's with.

Nodding, she takes the shirts and walks down the hall, her designer sandals snapping against the floor.

I watch her go. Sandy—Ms. Cunningham to all the parents—is wrangling her room of little ones, as are the other teachers. I don't get my own room until next week—I'm teaching pull-out art classes—so I'm wrangling the parents.

When I hear the Community Center's door whoosh open I look up, expecting another neighborhood mom to saunter in, or the second dad. We have two today. The first guy, a tech from one of the local computer businesses, walked in early, blinking like he'd never seen the sun before, and went about following directions as well as the best of our students. He waits now in his bright yellow t-shirt in his daughter's room helping the other kids with theirs.

The second one is little Bart's father. Sandy's eyebrow arched just a tad bit when she said his name, and her lips rounded for a fraction of a second. The man had a reputation—a *good* reputation.

I remember the news reports. How Bart's father and another firefighter got a family out of an apartment building before it collapsed. How they'd both been injured. Dan Quidell is a hero.

I'd seen Bart's file. Hell, all the teachers have seen his file. We need to know when kids have non-custodial parents who might cause problems and sadly, little Bart is one such kid. So I know what his dad looks like, as I do his ex-wife. Her photo in the file is a six-year old snapshot. His, a slightly blurry cell phone snap. Mr. Quidell holds Bart but he's turning away, like he doesn't want his photo taken. Bart, though, is mugging for the photographer, as Bart tends to do.

There'd been the snickers in the break room this morning when Sandy went over the parent list. "Hug a Teacher" mugs held high and the calls to make sure that when Dan Quidell changes into his neon colored parent t-shirt, he does it out in the open, where they all can see.

I rolled my eyes. Because, I'm sure, the man *likes* being considered a piece of meat. The disrespect left a sour taste.

But when the Community Center doors whoosh open and the road noise rolls in, when I see one Mr. Daniel Quidell in the flesh for the first time, only two words echo through my head. Two very unteacher-like words. Two words that sum up the halting physical grace before me: *Holy fuck.*

The sun backlights his body, so I can't immediately see his face, but I see his shape. Like a lot of tall men, he does the slight head duck as he walks across the threshold into the main lobby, even though he has plenty of clearance. He twists too, angling in one broad shoulder before the other.

He moves like the dancers I used to date, gliding on strong, sure legs. But I see the snagging of his joints, and, I suspect, some aches, and I'm sure not all his injuries healed right.

His scars from his firefighter days must still cause him pain.

Stopping just inside the door, under the full glory of the lobby's huge skylight, he curls one sculpted bicep as he reaches to pull off his sunglasses.

The tingle doesn't creep up from my belly or between my legs or from any other part of my body. It manifests from every one of my cells as if I'm standing between two static electricity generators. Two of those huge sparking monstrosities from old movies, the ones Dr. Frankenstein used to bring his monster to life.

I look at the big, gorgeous man framed by the Community Center's entrance, at his well-proportioned chest and arms, his flat abs and his strong, centered-though-pained gait as he walks toward me, and my entire body suddenly has a mind of its own. Or half a mind. It most certainly has *desire*.

Holy fuck bounces through my head again. I want to rub those shoulders. Soothe those aches. Stretch and loosen that body. I want to give him relief in *every* way possible.

He hooks one temple of his sunglasses over the collar of his long-sleeved t-shirt as he glances around. A smile appears as he notices my table. And me.

I hope I'm not blushing. God, I feel like I'm blushing. My skin feels hot and my nipples tingle and I swear if he asks, I'll sneak off to a supply closet with him just so I can suck him off.

Which is unprofessional of me. *Very* unprofessional. For goodness sake, I teach his little boy.

But the smiling Mr. Quidell, with his short chocolate brown hair and his incredible blue-green eyes, is beyond gorgeous.

He extends his hand. "Dan Quidell," he says, his voice washing over me in a wave of warm, deep tones. Damn it, he sounds as good as he looks.

One side of his mouth curls up higher than the other. Just a little, and it gives him a hint of devilishness. He's got a swashbuckling air to him, but in a leader kind of way, like he's the head pirate.

I inhale and stand up straight, determined to be professional. I will not embarrass myself and I most definitely will not embarrass a parent. I like my new job, even if I need to find a second one to pay my rent and my school loans. Losing the job I have because I'm an idiot is out of the question.

I take his hand, shaking once. His fingers are roughly smooth, with that thicker texture testosterone gives a man's skin, and they engulf mine.

I inhale again.

"Ms. Frasier." He nods toward my name tag and I swear his eyes are lingering on my chest. "You're new?" Oh, his voice really is like sonic velvet.

When he releases my hand, I almost sigh. His gaze does the unconscious dance over my breasts and my hips that straight men's eyes do, and it takes all my effort not to wiggle where I stand.

The man is too damned distracting.

But I think he's trying to be professional, too. Because I'm one of his kid's teachers.

"Started this week." I smile as I pretend to look for his name on the list. "I'll be teaching pull-out art classes as soon as my room is set up."

"Bart will like that."

I look up again. He's still smiling, but now the muscles of his face have taken on a deeper pull. His stance changed, too. I can't put my finger on it, but I'm sure, all the way to my bones, that this man loves his son.

And I want to sigh again, but I don't. I dig through the pile and pull out a neon pink, size medium t-shirt. "I have your t-shirt right here."

No way is it going to fit.

Mr. Quidell laughs when he holds it up. "We match."

He's right. I hadn't thought about it, but the store only had six colors, so there's doubling. Each teacher got a color and Sandy put one parent with most of us.

And I got Mr. Quidell.

I *am* blushing. I must be the same color as our shirts.

He's making a face and yanking on the seams of the shirt, like he's trying to stretch it. "Is this the biggest you have?"

"No one warned me about your big broad shoulders," I blurt out.

Oh hell, I think, and curl my lips into a thin line. I almost slap a hand over my mouth, but that would just make things worse.

He laughs again and that crooked smirk reappears—and my stray thought about vanishing into a supply closet with him for a quickie jumps back into my head.

Why am I thinking this way? I know how to keep my libido in check. I'm not some young freshman with a crush on the senior quarterback. Or a hero-worshipping fangirl.

The last thing he needs is to think that I'm some firefighter bunny.

His brow crinkles. His gaze drops away and he steps back, holding the t-shirt up between us like a screen. "I'll make do." When he lowers the t-shirt, he's looking down the hall. "Should I go to Bart's room?"

Did I make some unfriendly facial tic? Did he pick up something from my body language? I stiffen, thinking my ogling made him uncomfortable. He's a parent of one of my students. Damn it, I need to be professional.

Kids are so much easier to deal with than men.

I hand him his group's pink t-shirts and his list. "We'll be lining up in a couple of minutes. Will you be riding on the bus with us?"

He glances at the names before answering. "Had an indicator light come on as I was parking, so it looks like it." A frown jumps across his face before he flashes another friendly-but-distant smile.

I make a show of marking my sheet. Dan Quidell nods one more time, watching me for a longer moment than I expected, then walks away, toward his son....

THE STORY CONTINUES IN BOOK TWO, **DANIEL'S FIRE...**

●

THE WORLDS OF
KRIS AUSTEN RADCLIFFE

Hot Contemporary Romance:

The Quidell Brothers
Thomas's Muse
Daniel's Fire
Robert's Soul
Thomas's Need

Quidell Brothers Box Set
Includes:
Thomas's Muse
Daniel's Fire
Roberts's Soul

*Genre-bending Science Fiction about
love, family, and dragons:*

WORLD ON FIRE

Series one

Fate Fire Shifter Dragon

Games of Fate

Flux of Skin

Fifth of Blood

Bonds Broken & Silent

All But Human

Men and Beasts

The Burning World

Dragon's Fate and Other Stories

Series Two

Witch of the Midnight Blade

Witch of the Midnight Blade Part One

Witch of the Midnight Blade Part Two

Witch of the Midnight Blade Part Three

Witch of the Midnight Blade: The Complete Series

Series Three

World on Fire

Call of the Dragonslayer (*coming soon*)

Smart Urban Fantasy:

Northern Creatures

Monster Born

Vampire Cursed

Elf Raised

Wolf Hunted

Fae Touched

Death Kissed

God Forsaken
Magic Scorned
Witch Burned (*coming soon*)

Northern Creatures Box Set One: Books 1-3
Northern Creatures Box Set Two: Books 4-6

ABOUT THE AUTHOR

As a child, Kris took down a pack of hungry wolves with only a hard-cover copy of *The Dragonriders of Pern* and a sharpened toothbrush. That fateful day set her on a path traversing many storytelling worlds —dabbles in film and comic books, time as a talent agent and a text-book photo coordinator, and a foray into nonfiction. After co-authoring *Mind Shapes: Understanding the Differences in Thinking and Communication*, Kris returned to academia. But she craved narrative and a richly-textured world of Fates, Shifters, and Dragons—and unexpected, true love.

Kris lives in Minnesota with her husband, two daughters, Handsome Cat, and an entire menagerie of suburban wildlife bent on destroying her house. That battered-but-true copy of *Dragonriders*? She found it yesterday. It's time to pay a visit to the woodpeckers.

Fore more information
www.krisaustenradcliffe.com
krisradcliffe@sixtalonsign.com

www.ingramcontent.com/pod-product-compliance
Lightning Source LLC
Chambersburg PA
CBHW071406170626
46811CB00003B/1282